D0965606

A GRAVEYARD GOTHIC

by BILL RICHARDSON

illustrations by BILL PECHET

Thomas Dunne Books
St. Martin's Press ❦ New York

THOMAS DUNNE BOOKS.

An imprint of St. Martin's Press.

WAITING FOR GERTRUDE. Copyright © 2001 by Bill Richardson. Illustrations copyright © 2001 by Bill Pechet. All rights reserved. Printed in the United States of America. No part of this book may be used or reproduced in any manner whatsoever without written permission except in the case of brief quotations embodied in critical articles or reviews. For information, address St. Martin's Press, 175 Fifth Avenue, New York, N.Y. 10010.

www.stmartins.com

Design by Jacqueline Verkley

ISBN 0-312-31868-5

First published in Canada by Douglas & McIntyre

First U.S. Edition: October 2003

10 9 8 7 6 5 4 3 2 1

To K., who stands on guard

Acknowledgements

I would like to thank Scott McIntyre, Saeko Usukawa, Jacqueline Verkley and Kelly Mitchell. Thanks also to Denis Walz, to Robert Wyatt and especially to Bill Pechet, for his drawings, insights and the great pleasure of his company.

Portions of this book, in a very different form, first appeared in the *Georgia Straight*.

Catalogue of Players

(in order of appearance)

ALICE B. TOKLAS: Then, a cook and companion to Gertrude Stein. Now, a full-time waiter.

TRISTESSE: Her sister, a letter carrier in the employ of Chopin.

JIM MORRISON: Then, a rock star. Now, the embodiment of the male principle.

GERTRUDE STEIN: Then, a writer. Now, missing.

JEAN DE LA FONTAINE: Then, a fabulist. Now, a tour guide.

OSCAR WILDE: Then, a poet and playwright. Now, a *flâneur*.

ISADORA DUNCAN: Then, a dancer. Now, a dancer.

ROSSINI: Then, a composer. Now, an ageing bon vivant.

COLETTE: Then, a writer and mime. Now, a yoga instructor.

BONNE MAMAN: Then, a spiritualist. Now, a sorceress.

CHOPIN: Then, a composer. Now, Postmaster General.

ONDINE: A Planned Parenthood advocate.

MARIA CALLAS: Then, a singer. Now, a singer.

BARON HAUSSMANN: Then, an urban planner. Now, a demolitions enthusiast.

MODIGLIANI: Then, a painter. Now, a painter.

EDITH PIAF: Then, a cabaret artist. Now, a laundress.

SARAH BERNHARDT: Then, an actress. Now, an actress.

MARCEL PROUST: Then, a writer. Now, a private investigator.

BUTTONS: Miss Toklas's assistant.

HÉLOÏSE: Then, a nun, legendary lover and letter writer. Now, a society caterer and lifestyle consultant.

ABÉLARD: Then, an academic and lover of Héloïse. Now, a publicist.

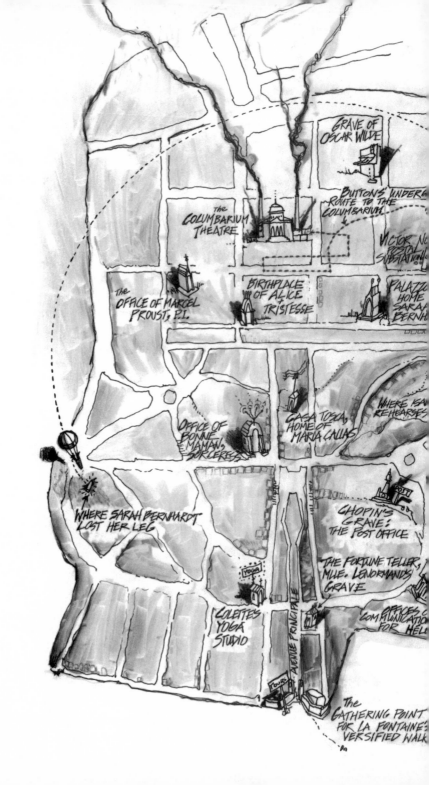

GRAVE OF
OSCAR WILDE

BUTTON'S UNDERG
ROUTE TO THE
COLUMBARIUM

THE
COLUMBARIUM
THEATRE

VICTOR N
POSTAL
SUBSTATION

THE
OFFICE OF MARCEL
PROUST, P.I.

BIRTHPLACE
OF ALICE
TRISTESSE

PALAZZ
HOME
SARA
BERNH

WHERE ISA
REHEARSES

OFFICE OF
BONNE
MAMAN,
SORCERESS

CASA TOSCA,
HOME OF
MARIA CALLAS

CHOPIN'S
GRAVE:
THE POST OFFICE

WHERE SARAH BERNHARDT
LOST HER LEG

THE FORTUNE TELLER,
MLLE. LENORMANDS
GRAVE

YOGA

OFFICES
COMMUNICATIO
FOR HEL

COLETTE'S
YOGA
STUDIO

AVENUE PRINCIPALE

TOUR

THE
GATHERING POINT
FOR LA FONTAINE
VERSIFIED WALK

GRAVE OF GERTRUDE STEIN
+ ALICE B. TOKLAS

HOME OF EDITH PIAF,
LAUNDRESS

WHERE ROSSINI LAUNCHED
THE BALLOON

WHERE ALICE + TRISTESSE
LIVE

WHERE ROSSINI
ENDS HIS DAYS

RIBBON
NCE

MORRISON'S GRAVE
'THE DRUGSTORE'

ÉLARD
TEST KITCHEN

LE
CIMETIÈRE
DU
PÈRE-LACHAISE

UR

"I like somebody being dead and how it moves along."

—Gertrude Stein, *Everybody's Autobiography*

Preamble

The first time I visited Père-Lachaise Cemetery was the first time I visited Paris. That was when I was twenty-one. Père-Lachaise is famous for the number and beauty of its monuments, and for the illustrious people buried or otherwise commemorated there. They include the composers Bizet, Chopin and Rossini, as well as any number of painters and sculptors. Seurat, Modigliani and Pissarro are there, along with such actors, dancers and entertainers as Isadora Duncan, Edith Piaf, Maria Callas, Sarah Bernhardt and Jim Morrison. Among the many writers are Balzac, Colette, Proust, Oscar Wilde and the fabulist Jean de La Fontaine. Gertrude Stein was buried there in 1946. Her companion, Alice B. Toklas, joined her in 1967. Theirs is a modest grave, especially by Père-Lachaise standards: a granite block carved with their names, one on either side, along with their dates of entry and exit. Gertrude's birthplace has been misspelled; Alice's inscription begins in English and ends in French.

Père-Lachaise has been sectioned off into ninety-seven different divisions dispersed over 114 acres. The divisions are really like neighbourhoods, and each, like any neighbourhood, has its own set of idiosyncrasies. Some are ancient, some more recent. Some are a jumble of tilted mausoleums; others are kept in neater trim. Some contain a heterogeneous mix of tenants; others are ethnically specific.

Not all the divisions are what you would call sedate. A carnival atmosphere prevails in the colourful 6th division, which is always crowded with fans of Jim Morrison. Once upon a time, members of the Lizard King's cult liked to leave graffiti traces of their passing. Now, guards stand by, ever on the alert for the telltale rattle of an aerosol can. Another breed of acolytes flocks to the 89th division to place tokens before the splendid art deco monument, sculpted by Jacob Epstein, that marks the final resting place of Oscar Wilde. The writer is portrayed as a winged, naked angel. When the statue was unveiled in 1914, it provoked great controversy, not so much because of the criminal history of the man it honoured but because of the size and the prominence of its manly endowment. In 1922, when the troublesome phallus was hacked away by vandals, a minor apocrypha was born. Some say the emasculation was the work of high-spirited students. Some say the unmanning was the work of a pair of offended Englishwomen. Some say that one of the custodians of Père-Lachaise recovered the lopped-off bits and used them as a paperweight. Their present whereabouts are a mystery.

In the 11th division, music lovers can dependably be found laying roses at the Chopin monument. Chopin's grave, who can say why, has also become the cemetery's unofficial post office. Over the years it has become traditional to leave letters there for one's beloved.

Père-Lachaise is my favourite place in all of Paris. My fondness was fixed on that first visit. It was late afternoon, a fine day, early in September. A time of lengthening shadows. I was wandering aimlessly among the antique stones, when a gnomish woman slipped from between two mausoleums, flagged me down and asked, *"Cherchez-vous Sarah Bernhardt?"* Clearly, she took a custodial interest in the great actress and had made it her particular mission to funnel tourists in Bernhardt's direction. As I had no agenda in mind, I was happy enough to follow the instructions, and I soon found the site. There, sitting sedately beside the Bernhardt grave, looking very much at ease, was a long-haired, grey cat, one of the sizable colony of feral cats that lives in the cemetery. She— I'm sure she was a she—had deep blue eyes and a proprietary air. She looked at me. I looked at her. We shared a moment of communion. Then she turned her attention to laundering a paw. I moved on. No doubt she put me from her mind straight away. But I never forgot her.

That elegant creature, and the other confident feral cats I saw going about their business in the cemetery, started me wondering what it would be like to inhabit the body of a cat. Furthermore, what if the souls of the late and great who are buried in Père-Lachaise were reincarnated in such a way? What tales would they have to tell about themselves and about each other? About life on four legs? The sentence "There was never such a ratter as Sarah Bernhardt" entered my head. I took my little notebook from my backpack. I wrote it down.

That was a long time ago, when I was young, when I was in Paris and in Père-Lachaise for the first time. That was when this story began.

Part I

November: Alice's Way

Alice B.

I was born in San Francisco, California. Then again, I was born in Paris, France. Paris, France, is also where I died. If one had to choose two cities in which to be born or in which to die, one could do worse than San Francisco, California, and Paris, France. Both have much to recommend them.

From the moment of my first birth in San Francisco—if something as heaving and as shuddering as a birth can be said to have taken place in "a moment"—and the moment of my dissolution in Paris—which fizzling also did not transpire with the insouciant swiftness of a finger snap—I made my way through the world on two legs.

Now I have four.

After my life on two legs ended and before my life on four began, there was a long stretch of stasis. I inhabited a treacle-coloured dominion, muffled and moist. A republic of indolent floating, with no view to speak of and little to watch or study, save for the slow, incessant leafing of an endless novel whose pages bore only one word:

Nothing.
  Nothing.
    Nothing.

And then, without warning, the word was made flash. There was an explosion of light, and my accustomed nothingness was no more. The abiding quiet was ruptured by a mew so monumental it might have been the outraged clamour of the unseaming earth; or so it seemed, at least, after that deep and attenuated silence. Imagine my surprise when I realized that the primal squeak that shattered the calm had erupted from my very own throat; to say nothing of how astonished I was to discover that, in the blink of an eye and without ever asking, I again *had* such a thing as a throat.

First there was light and then there was sound, and then

this modest *son et lumière* blossomed into heady sentience. My new lungs burned with the acid onslaught of oxygen. I felt the aggravated rasp of a tongue that was not my own, passing all up and down my untried flesh; a tongue that, between licks, was the engine of an embittered, plaintive litany.

"Kittens, kittens, kittens."

A voice both coarse and slatternly. My mother's voice.

"Kittens, kittens, kittens."

Anger and agony, mixed in equal measure.

"When will there be an end to these cursed kittens?"

The licking stopped, and I was shoved without ceremony onto a well-chewed teat. Appetite. How long had it been since I had had an appetite? I fastened my freshly minted mouth around the proffered nipple, but the wages of my sucking hardly repaid the effort, so meagre were they. So sour.

"Christ save me, here comes another!"

And as the hissing and moaning redoubled, a distant lamentation of church bells came walloping through the chill air, a tolling that bore on its back the certainty that I had crossed once more into the world of seconds and minutes and hours. Direct from the womb, a new exile from timelessness, I was teetering towards yet another death. And for better or worse, I had been given four legs to carry me there.

"*Bonjour,* Tristesse!"

This was my mother's plaintive cry as the eighth and final kitten shouldered her way out of the womb and jockeyed for position at the milk bar. *Tristesse.* Now, I understand that our mother was saluting Lady Sadness, the snaggle-toothed dame who was her midwife at this and all her other *accouchements.* But then, in my newborn innocence, I believed she was conferring a name on the last of the little mewlers. And so, Tristesse is what I christened her, and Tristesse is what she remains to this very day. To me she owes her name and to me she owes her life, for she had hardly attached herself to the last unclaimed nipple before the air was rent by a low rumble that was made of threat and danger.

I must interrupt the narrative at this thrilling juncture to note that when I was born in Paris, France—which is to say, when I was born with four legs rather than two—I was also born with eyes that were clear and open. There was nothing about them that was squinty or membranous. They were, from the very get go, ready to receive all the available light, primed to usher images from the outside world to the private cache that is my intellect, my memory. *Memories*, rather, for I have two discrete sets of recollections: one of life on two legs, and one of life on four, and they are layered within me, stratified and marbled, as though in a terrine. I forget nothing, not from that life and not from this, which is a blessing and a burden both. I remember looking up from our mother's arid dugs and reading the oracular inscription on the lofty tomb that cast a shadow over our natal bed:

NAÎTRE MOURIR RENAÎTRE ENCORE ET PROGRESSER SANS CESSE
TELLE EST LA LOI.

Here, writ large, was the answer to the riddle of my being, the succinct summation of the universal principle that held me in its thrall. *To be born, to die, to be born again, and to be forever moving on. This is the law.*

I remember this, just as clearly as I remember our mother's meowling, remember her calling out "Tristesse," and then the throat-born thunder that made me look up and around and directly into the bloodshot eyes of Morrison.

"Well, well," said our mother, "if it isn't the Lizard King himself."

He growled again, but sweet somehow, like honey oozing miraculously from a boulder, a murderous seduction.

"Help yourself, Lizard King," she said, heaving herself up from her bed of pain and dislodging the suckers to whom she gave succour. "Help yourself and welcome to them. Christ knows you'll be doing us all a favour. The last thing the world needs is more damn kittens."

And then she wandered off. She left him to it. He wasted no time laying waste to the litter. It was only because of my eyes that I survived to tell the tale and that I was exempt from his gnashing and devouring. When his eyes and my eyes met, he knew me as one whose birth was crowned with purpose, knew that I had been born to fulfil some manifestation of The Law. He knew that it would be an unpardonable crime to come between me and my mission here. So blunt and so upper case a capper as *TELLE EST LA LOI* leaves very little room for equivocation.

So I was spared. As for Tristesse, she was saved because some self-preserving instinct made her squirm her blind way into the shelter of my lee, and I could think of no good reason to betray her to Morrison's ravages. Spill of blood, crush of bone, tear of flesh: in the end, only we two remained.

"Lucky for you he's such a picky eater," said our mother, when she returned to survey the carnage. She had just enough grudging maternal instinct left in her to nurse us for the first few critical weeks. Then came the morning that she went out ratting and never returned.

"We're on our own," I said to Tristesse, who trembled so violently at the news of our abandonment that I didn't have the heart to cast her loose. She has clung to me with burr-like tenacity ever since, and every morning when I salute her—"*Bonjour*, Tristesse"—I greet not only my sister but also my own sadness. Every morning I begin anew the business that has brought me here, which is the patient and pulse-slowing business of merely waiting. Waiting for my joy, my love, my baby. Waiting for my Gertrude.

In one way or another, in one life or another, I have been waiting a very long time. I never imagined, during the gilded days of our protracted co-tenancy, when Gertrude Stein wrote and when I, Alice B. Toklas, stood guard, that it would come to this. I never imagined that she would die first, that I would stay on alone, a widow, for twenty more years, dancing my limping and solitary two-step. I never imagined that, in the immediate aftermath of my own snuffing, the essential, animating part of me—oh, let's just call it a soul—would detach as easily as any breath, divest itself of its flesh and fluid, and float about in a place of muted otherness, like a blinking satellite programmed for eventual re-entry; nor that, in answer to some ineffable imperative, I would come crashing to earth in the body of a cat—a failure of imagining that is perhaps a pardonable lapse—and that I would find myself, once again, alone. Which is not to say that I have been without company. Mercy, no! There are plenty of us four-legged ones here in Père-Lachaise. Wilde. Bernhardt. Callas. Colette. Rossini. Proust. The guest list is glittering. It would be hard to imagine a more cunningly curated community, but a vital component is missing: Gertrude, the one piece I uniquely require to become the whole and real me. Gertrude, the shining alpha to balance my dark omega, who was for forty years my husband.

For months after my advent, while I adapted to whiskers and to tail, I fumed at the injustice of her absence. I stamped. I ranted. Not fair! Not fair! Not fair! I exhausted myself with outrage, tormented myself with untoward fantasies: that she had come and gone, that she had found another, that she had trod a different transmigratory path altogether and had slipped into the flesh of a dung beetle or a donkey.

I teetered on the cusp of madness until the day I was invaded—who can say why—by a fierce and sudden calm. An Old Testament kind of voice boomed in the vault of my skull. *"She will come,"* it said. *"She will come."* And those three syllables echoed with such lordly authority that I understood, with a shameful clarity, how all my doubting had been wrong, need-less, diminishing. Flushed with assurance and pulled from the slough by a green and vibrant confidence, I knew, for certain and all at once, that our love was solid, an immutable force in the ever-expanding universe, and that she, my brave salmon, would fight her way up any stream in order to make her way home to me. My only responsibility was to wait and to refine my waiting; to study forbearance and to believe that, in the fullness of time, my faith would be rewarded.

She will come, she will come, and I will bask in her particular incandescence; for when she comes, she will shine with that selfsame light that illumined my salad days, and her light will not be any the dimmer for all its years of concealment, which cannot be said for most of the writers who are here among us. Many sustained damaged over the period of their storage or during the transfer. They have been spindled, folded and mutilated to such an extent that some, however glorious they might once have been, now belong to a decidedly ersatz rank. La Fontaine is a case in point. He comes to mind because now, as I look from my window, I see him, our versifying tour guide, making his way down the path towards my house, shepherding his flock of four-footed looky-loos, wide-eyed and gullible, spicing his spiel with who knows what lies. Tourists! They are a bane.

Time for me to make myself scarce. Time for me to make myself ready. Soon she will come, my love, my puss. She will come, and my long widowhood will end. She will come and she will find me here, waiting, waiting. Waiting for Gertrude.

LA FONTAINE'S VERSIFIED WALKING TOUR: WELCOME

Welcome, cats. I offer thanks—
Tabby, ginger, Persian, Manx,
Tortoiseshell and coal-vein black,
Plump of belly, sleek of back,
Eyes of copper, eyes of green,
Randy tom and preening queen—
Welcome, stray and purest bred,
To this playground of the dead,

Welcome to this yard of bones.
Please turn off all pagers, phones,
Render mute whatever might
Rend our sacred, silent night.

Excellent. Now let's be sure,
As we start this guided tour,
Creeping forth on velvet paws,
Everyone has come because
They've a hunger they must sate
Here among the late and great.
If you tag along with me,
Having paid a modest fee,
You shall, for this evening, bide
Where Parisian greats who died
Came to rest, not knowing that
They would be reborn as cats.

Sages wise have often taught,
When the body starts to rot,
That the soul from flesh is pried,
Then is changed, transmogrified.
And they're right. It happens thus:
Shortly, and with little fuss,
When one's breath has finally failed,
One appears again, be-tailed.
Some will bellow, "That's absurd!
First interred and then be-furred?"
But it's true. Hence, I was born
La Fontaine in feline form.

What, one wonders, would they say,
Bernhardt, Balzac, or Bizet,
Had they known the final score:
Two legs one day, next day four?

How would they have laid their bets,
Chopin, Callas, or Colette,
Had they known their future role
Would entail a taste for vole?
Would they weep or would they laugh,
Proust and Poulenc and Piaf,
At the thought of eating mouse?
Would they grin? Or would they grouse?

Oscar Wilde, Seurat, Molière:
Check the roster, all are there,
Deepening their catlike ways
On the grounds of Père-Lachaise.
Celebrity's a shiny lure,
You shall meet some on this tour—
All save Gertrude. I'm afraid
That *grande dame* has been delayed.
Gertrude who? Why, Gertrude Stein.
Poor Miss Toklas! How she pines,
Exiled from her land of bliss,
Aching for her husband's kiss.

Questions? Yes, there, on the right.
Ah. You wonder if the night
Is riskless, safe, hazard-free?
This, I cannot guarantee.
By and large, though, not to fret,
Not one tourist's perished yet.
Should the Lizard King arise,
Caution then I might advise.
Ready, then? Fine. Let's begin.
Welcome, cats! Cats, welcome in.

⚜

LETTER: OSCAR WILDE TO JIM MORRISON

October 31

Dear Heart:
Something is in the air, Jamz. Something is about to happen.
Can you sniff its musky imminence? So tense and delicious.
So ejaculatory and on the verge. As if the whole of Père-
Lachaise is hanging on the cusp of a tremendous sneeze. We
are teetering on the dangerous edge of something big, Jamz,
and I am bound to say that teetering is not easy for me, given
the present tenderness of my paws, which are as pink and
shredded as the eraser of some overreaching scribe. And what
have I been hoping to rub out? Nothing but your stubborn,
lamentable absence, Jamz. Nothing but that.

In heaven's name, where are you? All day long I have
searched for you, all day long walked the length and breadth
of the cemetery, skirting its margins, navigating its byways,
stumping over its coarse brick roadways, but found you not.
Up and down I sallied, all along the major arteries and minor
capillaries of Père-Lachaise, turning right, turning left on
the chemin Gosselin and the chemin d'Ornano, the chemin
Errazu and the avenue des Peupliers. And what prize, what
merit badge did I earn, for having so painfully subverted my
slothful nature and subscribed to these perverted acts of
exertion? Not a one. You have been resolute in your invisi-
bility. There was not a single sighting.

Others were out and about. I saw Isadora, that arrested
adolescent, trailing her ribbons and chasing her tiger-stripe
tail. I saw the one-eyed Rossini, huge and white and ancient,
more doddering than ever, sitting all alone, chatting amiably
to an imaginary companion. I observed and ignored the harridan Colette, who since her arrival has loved nothing more
than to taunt me and who would surely have hurled some
barbed jibe my way had she detected my passing. Fortunately,
she has taken up yoga and was, quite literally, too wrapped up

in herself to pay me any mind. By the time she had solved the Gordian knot of her own limbs, I was out of sight and migrating north.

I walked where the tight ranks of ancient ossuaries are falling into disrepair, leaning precariously, one against the other, like overcrowded teeth. (Indeed, they bear a striking resemblance to the mouth of a boy I knew in another place and another time; one who disappeared without a word, but not before I had taken care of his dental bills.) I walked among lofty mausoleums and merely utilitarian scatters of stones and took note of the various names inscribed on the various tombs. Yilmaz. Guney. Bottelier. Mazaud. Dulac. Perrin. On tiny temples and towering obelisks, on lofty columns and polished whacks of granite, I saw Le Floch, Dufour, Joule, Tissier, Huet, Boulanger. I read the chiselled catalogue of the Parisian dead with no more interest than I might have brought to a perusal of the telephone directory, for there was only one name I wanted to see made flesh. James. Jimmy. Jim-Boy. Jamz.

Père-Lachaise, it must be said, is a better bargain for those who hide than for those who seek. The narrow lanes, the awkward angles, the sudden gullies and unexpected hollows, the shadow-thin spaces between the tombs: these accommodate the fast absorption of those who are both sinewy and determined not to be found.

"Come out, come out, wherever you are!" I carolled, to no good effect, as I circumnavigated the columbarium and crematorium—a telltale plume hanging prettily above the chimney—and sliced a diagonal line through the 90th division, tripping over the lumpen grotesque called Bonne Maman. The witch was hunkered between two granite slabs—they were only marginally more slabby than she, I have to tell you—and she was culling the various pulses and simples she requires for her spell-casting. Little wonder that I didn't see her. Her coat—a variegated variation on the colour brown—was like camouflage gear.

"Watch it, oaf," she hissed, collecting her mottled mass.

I would have answered in kind, did I not suspect that there is more to Bonne Maman than girth and wind. I think it possible, Jamz, that she is the genuine item: that she is, in fact, the sorceress she claims to be. Miss Toklas swears by her powers, and Miss Toklas, while hopeless in some regards, is by and large nobody's fool. I swallowed my cutting riposte and helped Bonne Maman gather up her vegetative bits, of which there were more than a few.

"Heavens," I said, as we piled her wicker trug with roots, leaves, twigs, seeds and bits of bark, "are you planning on weaving a wreath?"

"Mind your own damn business," she snapped, reflexively, and then took a baby step backwards into what passes, for her, as civility.

"Client confidentiality," she grumbled, prising a ribbon of moss from a sorry-looking headstone. Thus dismissed, I took my leave, zigzagging to the avenue Carette, thence to the 89th division and, finally, to the monument that marks the place where rests all that remains of my two-legged self. There, at last, exhaustion caught up with me. I found a sheltered spot in which to lie, then contemplated my memorial, as I have often done: the sculpted limestone angel, naked and full-lipped, with shuttered eyes and folded wings, poised either for dreaming or for flight. Poised, perhaps, for both. Whoever would have guessed, in the world of upright walking, that one would one day have the narcissistic pleasure of studying one's own tomb? It is so beautiful, Jamz. Someday, I would like to show you how beautiful it is. I would also show you how, like every lovely thing, it is flawed. Once, a long time ago, some passer-by—possessed of both a blunt instrument and the blunt certainty that angels must be sexless—took it upon herself to knock away the statue's sculpted manhood.

While such vandalism—to say nothing of such misplaced propriety—is always to be decried, that jagged scar only deepens my sense of connection with my own memorial. As you may know, Jamz, I have been similarly dismantled. I know well enough how it happened but could not tell you when, as I have blotted out any memory of that enforced excision. I am reminded of it, and I give an involuntary shudder, every time I lift my hind leg and indulge in a moment of nether cleansing. Whether the angel winced at the moment of emasculation, no one can tell. Nor can anyone say what became of the plundered petsie. For years it was reliably known that one of the groundskeepers kept the fruit of that harsh harvest on his desk as a paperweight. Then, it disappeared. The fate of the fallen phallus—I have heard whispers that it is now in the keeping of Bonne Maman, who uses it as a talisman for her occult extravaganzas—does not weigh so very heavily on me. It is not an artifact of Elgin marbles-like import. Its present co-ordinates are of little genuine concern in the *hic et nunc*.

Poor Jamz. You know no Latin, do you? You could. I could teach you. I could teach you Latin and much more besides. True, you give the superficial impression of being an unbreachable amalgam of sculpted musculature and brutish physicality, but I know there is more to you than that breathtakingly beautiful, Bernini-like surface. I have studied the swinging mass that is your bushel, and I know that a light shines beneath it. You may be a lump of unmoulded clay, but you are ripe for the kneading. And may I knead you, Jamz? I am ready. I am willing. I am your faithful eunuch.

I am, your ever adoring,
O.W.

ALICE B.

The good news about taking up residence in a cemetery is that there is plenty to read. Here, in Père-Lachaise, there are thousands upon thousands of monuments, memorials of every size and description, all of them inscribed with texts that attest to the qualities of the worthies whose mulch they mark. The bad news is that there is very little that is sustaining and that there is a certain stylistic sameness to these elegiac summations. Some bespeak an absurd, even a boastful, optimism, not even in the prospect of a happy afterlife but rather in the possibility that a minor legacy to humanity will live on and on:

> *We are aware that we have served a great cause, and we shall remain its servant. We shall leave open our windows, the better to hear the cries of the oppressed, the moans of the victims.*

Many have the shopworn sentiments of a bargain-basement epitaph:

> *How beautiful the feet of the angel who comes to announce my death.*

And still others are self-flagellating quotations cribbed from such cheerful sources as Job and Ecclesiastes:

> *Vanity of vanities, all is only vanity*

one reads, over and over, in imposing scripts chiselled deeply into the resistant grains of marble, of granite. These words are offered to the passer-by as a cautionary tale, as if vanity were something to be expiated, avoided at all costs; as if it were not as vital to continuance as a pulse. Often, vanity is all that keeps us going, and I can assure you that one of the final thoughts to gain purchase in the crumbling mind, as the last of its circuits explodes, is: *How do I look?* Take it from me. I have been there. I should know.

Vanity, vanity. In that other life, in that other time, my hands bore the brunt of my vanity. My face might not have launched a single ship, but, oh, the care I lavished on my manicure! The filing and the paring. The buffing and the varnishing. In this life, as in that, I am attentive to my hands; at least, to what I once called my hands. In this life, as in that, I cannot bear to have them soiled, and just at the moment they are filthy. Filthy! They are tainted with time. Little wonder. Devote yourself to the act of waiting and you'll end up with time on your hands, your paws, whatever your appendages. Sticky, staining time. How to wash the stuff away?

The old-fashioned remedies are best, I find. These include such reliable standbys as cooking, writing, meandering, visiting, gossiping. Also, I enjoy reading the correspondence of others. Over time, meddling with the mail has become one of my needs and specialties. I do it not just out of catlike curiosity and to redress the grimness of reading material hereabouts but also as a way of gathering intelligence, of ensuring that my purpose is edging towards fulfilment.

By way of example, consider dear Oscar's slavering Halloween missive to Morrison. You may think it speaks ill of me that I have betrayed a friend by waylaying his love letter, but my larceny is larded with benignity. I have done nothing to interfere with his deepest requirement, which is the venting of amatory steam; the note's composition was, I can say with surety, sufficient to satisfy that need. And its delivery would have been wholly superfluous and without outcome, for Morrison has never attained even the lowest plateau of literacy. It would have been a dreadful waste to disburse to him Oscar's thoughtfully written and very nicely punctuated pleadings. Better they should stay with me, so that I may comb them for signs that all is proceeding as it ought and that my best-laid plans are in no danger of going anywhere astray.

That voice that rang through the rafters of my noggin—*she will come, she will come*—seems to have dislodged flights of batty dreams. They lob their sonar cryptograms back and forth while I sleep. I cannot close my eyes without seeing Gertrude. She comes to me in the dreamtime mail. She slides down the dreamtime chimney. She rolls out of the dreamtime oven, toasty warm and sweet and ready to eat. The message is clear: she is, at last, ready to join me here in Père-Lachaise. My responsibility is to maximize the chance that she will find a port of entry. How best to arrange this?

"Ahhhhh," said the sorceress Bonne Maman, when I put the question to her, for I sensed that the assistance I required was as much astrological as it was actuarial.

"Ahhhhh," she said, as if I had just set before her a plate of freshly baked cinnamon rolls.

"Ahhhhh," and I could sense that she was warming to the challenge, to say nothing of the prospect of earning a quantity of the doctored dainties which have become my currency here. "Let me see what I can do."

"Something is in the air," intuited Oscar. "Something is about to happen." He is so right. The cogs and flywheels are about to mesh, and if all goes according to plan, theirs will not be the only grinding. If all goes according to plan, there will soon be many collisions of eligible loins in this kingdom of stone and bone and moan; a crying and a howling and a scattering of seed. What better place for a seed to take hold than atop this illustrious compost bin? Soon, if I can believe the counsel of dreams and the prognostications of my guts, a kitten called Gertrude will arrive to join our household. A kitten to rule the roost! And how, I wonder, will Tristesse take to that?

A word or two more about Tristesse. My sister. My millstone. My secret source of mail. Tristesse is a nice girl, but her wick could stand some trimming. She is more soot than light. The other day we were enjoying a little chinwag, just we two, and I was moved to say, "Isn't it amusing, Tristesse, that here we are, having a chat, and that *chat* is the word for 'cat' in the lingua franca of this place? What do you make of that?"

Her only response was a nervous shifting of the eyes, a puzzled grimace, as though she detected the beginnings of toothache but couldn't determine where in her mouth lay the source of the pain. So typical. When I talk to Tristesse, I feel like an artillery gunner whose every cannon is calibrated to overshoot the mark.

Chat = cat. A rudimentary act of translation. When all is said and done, it is translation that is the reason for our being. Our raison d'être. It is only the prospect of Gertrude's translation, from word into flesh, that buoys my days. For once she is flesh, we will pick up our words where last we left off. When we had four legs between us instead of four legs each. When she translated me and I translated her. I was the only one who could unravel the knot of her hand-writing. On late spring days, when the weather was fine and the chestnut trees moaned with the weight of their blossoms and the windows of our apartment were open wide, passers-by on the rue de Fleurus heard the steady *thwack-thwack* of my Smith as I cracked the code of her spidery cuneiform, con-verting into typescript the convoluted overflow of her heart. Likewise, she interpreted me, never more so than when she undertook my autobiography.

The Autobiography of Alice B. Toklas. It was Gertrude who wrote it, as everyone knows. Even so, "autobiography" is no misnomer, for my story was her story, and the words she put in my mouth were my own heartfelt words. I remember how she wrote that I had a gift for recognizing genius; that when a genius passed into my orbit, a bell within me rang. And that was true, long, long ago. Now, however, it is not the certainty of genius that rings the bell within. Rather, it is the recognition of a transla-tion that prompts tintinnabulation.

By "translation," I mean those who once walked the earth on two legs but who, in this life, have been given the gift of an extra pair. I am a translation, and Gertrude, when she arrives, will be a translation too. There will be no doubt in her mind that this is so, for no one needs to tell a translation that a translation is what she is. We know it of ourselves, instinctively and intuitively, just as we know it of others whenever our paths cross. When one translation meets another, there is a shiver of mutuality, as though you have intersected with someone who is carrying the same book and who at that very moment is reading the same words on the same page.

Morrison is a translation, and I knew it right away, just as I knew it of Rossini and Wilde and Bernhardt; just as I knew it of my very own mother, come to that. Yes, she is a translation, too, but her story, which is not uncluttered, I shall save for another time. Why it should be that some cats are animated by spirits that have walked the earth before, and some cats are cats, plain and simple, is a mystery. I am not privy to what goes on at that level of decision-making. I only know that it is so.

"Is she a translation?" was the first question Chopin asked me when I approached him, in his capacity of Postmaster General, about some simple but meaningful work for which Tristesse might be qualified and which would liberate me from her constant company.

"I'm afraid not. However, she is a hard worker and—"

"Not a translation is an advantage as far as I'm concerned. Less chance the worker will get caught up in the glory days of the past. Montand was here for a while, and he was hopeless, just hopeless. 'Yves,' I would say, 'your mission is to sort the mail and deliver it, not to strike one provocative pose after another.' Time and again I warned him, but it did no good, no good at all. Finally, I had to let him go."

"I think you'll find Tristesse rather more compliant."

"Then send her by. We'll see how it goes."

That was my first foray into vocational matchmaking, and I am very glad I took the initiative. It has worked out well for all concerned. I have secured the considerable consolation of blessed solitude while Tristesse is at work. She has prospered under a 9-to-5 regime, and her employment package comes with interesting benefits. Untrammelled access to her mailbag is a perk I would sorely miss, should she be found wanting and let go. Luckily, Chopin is, so far, without complaint, and my intelligence-gathering proceeds apace.

Chopin, Chopin, the despondent old Pole cat! Night after night he sits outside his house and sings his melancholy songs. Night after night he sits and sings, even when the weather has gone dank and chill, as it has now. As it properly should. This is Paris. This is November. And soon, Gertrude will be here. Soon, she will come.

⚜

Chopin: Nocturne for the Feast Day of All Saints

The sun sets. Dusk comes to Père-Lachaise. Now it is time for the two-legged living to be gone.

Sun sets, dusk comes, and the custodians make their customary sweep, from north to south to east to west, alert for distracted dalliers; for giggling dare-takers conniving to spend the night. The guards take their whistles and sound the note warning that soon the gates will be closed and bolted. A shrill note, a hemi-demi-semitone on the underside of F sharp. Theirs is a simple song, a one-note song, with melancholy words:

> *Get you gone, now, get you gone,*
> *You curious, aimless and mourning ones.*
> *Get you gone, now, get you gone.*
> *Come now, night. Now night, come on.*

Dusk comes. Whistles blow. I watch the slow outward migration of those who belong to the world beyond our walls: the celebrity seekers, the Gothic explorers, the newly bereaved and the ancestor worshippers. I watch for Ondine. She is always the last to leave. Old Ondine, with her crook of a back and her thin blue smock that she wears in all weathers. Dependable Ondine, with her tattered umbrella and her gunny sacks over her shoulders.

Chopin, in mid-Nocturne

Ondine comes every day with her bags full of food: thick cream and fragrant liver and chicken all diced up fine and savoury ragouts and an assortment of kibble, which is dry and vile but will do in a pinch. Every day she comes and distributes her largesse among the cats of Père-Lachaise; and every night, when the whistles blow, she leaves again, with those same gunnies over her shoulders. Often, they are not empty, those sacks. Often, she is carrying a couple of cats as baggage. A day or two later she returns them, and when they come home they are dazed and achy and deaf to the procreative siren songs that once tempted them onto the rocky shoals of romance. Somewhere in the world outside, at the hands of Ondine or of her agents, they have experienced the excision of desire.

Old Ondine, bent of back and tattered of arm and bloody of hand. Many a claw has raked her, from elbow to wrist to fingernail, but still she persists in her feeding and culling. She is a woman with a mission. A woman who will not be deterred. A woman who needs no armour other than the breastplate of her own righteousness. She cannot know—she has no way of knowing—that she has become a mythic figure in the folklore of this place. Mothers, sucked dry and exhausted and wanting only to calm their querulous kits, will invoke her name.

"Quiet," they will whisper. "Ondine is about. Ondine will hear. She'll throw you in her sack, and then where will you be? Then what will you do?"

Silence falls. Kittens sleep. They dream dire dreams. When they grow up, they will learn, some to their peril, that Ondine is more than a rumour. She is a bogey made of flesh and purpose. Her life is ruled by a simple equation: food + trust = pounce. She applies it rigorously. It has served her well, but many cats are canny. Keen of eye and ear and nose, and possessed of an occult wiliness, they take her bait, then beat a hasty retreat when she moves in for the grab. Bernhardt, Colette, Callas: they are too worldly by far to step into Ondine's snare. Nor is she likely to snag Morrison. Morrison would be her prize catch. Morrison, the indefatigable inseminator, the proud possessor of six-toed paws and a testicular triumvirate. Morrison, the preening juggler of three heavy balls, who spreads his seed as easily and as dispassionately as a newsboy hurls the morning papers. Even if Morrison knew how to count, he could never number his spawn.

Ondine is a crusader and Morrison is her Holy Grail, elusive, forever out of reach. He loves to toy with her, to tease her and tempt her. It has gone on like this for years. She doesn't stand a chance. She must console herself with those she is able to dupe: with Abélard, for instance, or with Oscar. Poor Wilde! He is destined, it seems, whatever his form, to fall victim to unsexing forces.

Now and then it happens that there is a rare cat who will willingly give herself or himself over to Ondine's mercies, which are anything but tender. Miss Toklas was such a one. "Because I want nothing of toms," was all the explanation she offered when she returned to us, spayed and sore. "Because I am good for one thing only. Because I am waiting for Gertrude."

Dusk has gone. Dark has come. The crows have clocked out. The owls have begun their shifts. Ondine has returned to the city beyond our city. I saw her pass, her sacks all slack, her eyes downcast. No matter. She shall have better days. As shall we all. In some distant division, Morrison is warming up for a long night of howling. I can hear him singing his scales. Flat. He is always dreadfully flat. Tune him out, Chopin. To work, to work. The midnight mail is piling fast, for dusk has gone and dark has come. For night is here at last.

❧

LETTER AND INVOICE: BONNE MAMAN TO ALICE B. TOKLAS

November 1

Dear Miss Toklas:

As per your request and our recent conversation, I have pre-pared an "Invocation for the End of Waiting." As we agreed, and as every sign suggests an auspicious outcome, I will enact it at midnight on All Souls' Eve.

I have taken the liberty of enclosing an invoice for services rendered, payable upon completion of the assignment. The agreed-upon fee reflects the attached schedule, which includes parts and labour.

I trust you will find that all is in order. Do not hesitate to contact me should you have any questions or concerns. I wish you all the very best with your enterprise. I am glad to have been of service.

Yours very truly,
Bonne Maman, Sorceress

Invoice
Bonne Maman Ventures, Inc.

Client Consultation	*2 hours*
Gathering of Materials	*5 hours*
Powering the Petsie	*12 hours*
Writing and Reciting of Invocation (enclosed)	*1 hour*
Total Time	*20 hours*

Invocation for the End of Waiting

I'm foreman and boss of the graveyard shift,
So listen to what I say.
I order you, spirits, your loins now lift,
Your marmoreal thighs now splay.
I order all fires of the deepest earth
And flames from remotest suns
Forge every binding to hasten the birth,
Engender the promised one.

Bind mortar to pestle!
Bind scabbard to sword!
Bind Tab A to Slot B!
Bind arch unto trestle!
Bind flesh unto word!
Bind shore unto crashing sea!

Howl by the light of the gibbous moon,
Howl through the snarl of snow.
Howl, for the night will be over too soon,
The petsie will cease to glow.

Be now regenerate!
Passions be lit!
Blood unto blood now be drawn!
Damn all profundity!
Bring on fecundity!
Howl till the light of the dawn!

Bonne Maman Ventures, Inc. Serving the Père-Lachaise Community for over fifteen years.

❖

ALICE B.

It is done. The yowling lasted all the livelong night. The din was music to my ears. Tristesse, I am sorry to say, did not find the concert as satisfying.

"Mademoiselle Alice! Will those rogues and harlots never pack it in?"

Tristesse hates it when her good night's sleep is trampled on. She claims she cannot function if she is less than fully alert. To hear her talk, you might think her a surgeon or an admiral, or perhaps the operator of some imposing and potentially lethal piece of industrial machinery, rather than a letter carrier, conscientious in the execution of her duties but, on the whole, uninspired.

"Such a carrying-on!" she prissed, then added, "Why, it's enough to wake the dead." She fired off this last salvo with the self-satisfied gusto of one who is oblivious to irony.

"Enough to wake the dead!" she repeated, savouring every syllable. Apparently, the little smile of acknowledgement I sent her way was insufficient reward for such brilliance.

"Enough to wake—"

"Thank you, Tristesse," I cut in, rather more sharply than I'd intended. "I heard you the first time."

Which set her to sulking. She pouted for hours until, finally, exhausted by the wearing combination of arch originality and deep indignation, she dozed. She snored.

Not I. I stayed awake, listening to that cathartic symphony, as elemental and rampaging as a fierce thunderstorm. Not until after 6 A.M. did the caterwauling dwindle and the pitched cries die away. Then, at last, I slept. I dreamed. I dreamed of Gertrude. I dreamed of her packing a bag, buying a ticket, catching a train. I dreamed of her, confident and ample, passing through the gates of this teeming necropolis, ascending my steps, lifting the knocker on my door, which is her door, also. But when I hurried to answer, I saw nothing but snow, silent and heavy, falling everywhere; and every flake was identical, and every flake was a frame for her face. The sky

was full of Gertrude Stein, and Gertrude Stein was everywhere, but Gertrude Stein was nowhere to be seen.

When finally I woke—it was well after noon—I was troubled,
exhilarated and surprised to see, looking out my window, that
sleep had made me a prophet and that snow was indeed falling,
thick and fast. Tristesse, dumbly obedient to her pledge that
no elemental inconvenience would impede her appointed
rounds, was somewhere out in the tempest, ferrying the mail.
She would return wet and exhausted and brimming with
inflated accounts of her bravery.

November 2. Early for snow. An aberrant flurry in this
place of mostly rain. All Souls' Day, in Père-Lachaise, is typically moist with mist. Mourners, freighted with flora, flock
to festoon the tombs. They look like grey ghosts as they shred
the frangible brume. By their thousands they come, laden
with the chrysanthemums that, for the French, are *de rigueur*
on this solemn day. They come with their flowers and lay
them down. They bow their heads and say their prayers.
Then, mindful of life's transience, they repair to a warm
bistro to reap the tangible benefits of flesh ownership.

By the time I had performed my ritual ablutions,
smoothed my whiskers and gathered up my casserole, the
families of the dead had come and gone. I imagined, given
that the fabled snows of yesteryear had rudely invaded the
here and now, that the pious bereaved might have been
hastier than usual in their observances; and, indeed, I had to
look carefully for any trace of their passing. The snow had
replenished the hollows of their footprints. It had obscured
their wreaths of white and braided blossoms.

The chrysanthemum inspires in me nothing but impa-
tience. Apart from its unfortunate role as Ambassador to
Mortality, it is burdened with a kind of chummy muscularity
that is unbecoming in flora. Nonetheless, I am bound to
admit that its brutishness serves it well when times are tough,
and as I negotiated the drifts, picking my way towards the
home of the sorceress, Bonne Maman, I picked a few of the
hardier heads and made a *faute de mieux* bouquet.

"For you, Madame," I said to the witch when she opened her door.

"You're late."

"The weather—" I began, but she was in no mood to brook excuses. Ignoring the flowers, she seized the casserole dish and lifted the lid to inhale its fragrance, both bitter and savoury, its aromatic wafts of artichoke and vole. Somewhat placated, she stepped aside to admit me into her squalid den. A single candle burned on her makeshift altar, casting flickering shadows on her collection of stones and bones, on her random assembly of reeds and beads, on all her sundry tools of divination. Rising above them, like a sausage balanced between two eggs, was the most treasured of her talismans, the tumescent source of all my hope: Oscar's severed stone petsie.

"And where," spat Bonne Maman, "is my sweet?"

"Proof before cake."

"What about our bargain?"

"I've not forgotten the arrangement, Madame: your spell in exchange for my cuisine. But how do I know it worked?"

Her orange eyes blazed and she shook her twisted mane.

"Did it work? Haven't you ears, girl? Weren't they at it all night long? Have you ever heard such a brouhaha?"

She nodded in the direction of the sculpted shaft that occupies so proud a place of prominence among her grisly souvenirs.

"You should have seen how it glowed bright red from dusk till dawn. Why, I could have roasted chestnuts over it, it was that hot. Come New Year's Day, you won't be able to take a step without treading on kindles of kittens."

"But will *she* be among them?"

"Don't ask foolish questions. How would I know?"

"You're a witch, aren't you? Use your crystal ball, your deck of cards, your tea leaves."

"There's no one but Time can tell you what you want to hear, as I've said to you before, and more than once, too. Now, give me my sweet and be on your way. And take those damn flowers with you."

"Have it then," I hissed, hurling the coveted cake over her head and into a cobwebbed corner. I had the satisfaction of watching her indecorous scrambling as she dove under the table to retrieve it. All that was visible of her, as I turned to go, was her fat and matted rear, wiggling as she scrabbled after her prize.

I made my way home through the dull and talkative tumble of snow. *La neige, la neige, la neige,* it seemed to whisper, over and over and over. *She will, she will, she will,* it sang, and my heart joined in the chorus with its persuasive, percussive, *come, come, come.* And so it has begun, the season of Gertrude's nurturing; and soon it will end, my long, long wait.

⚜

ALICE B. COOKS: ALL SOULS' CAKE

This simple confection—the very sweet so craved by the degenerate Bonne Maman—is a traditional treat for this time of year. It is simplicity itself to prepare.

You will require a cake of yeast and some warm water in which to dissolve it, sugar, butter—half a cup of each is recommended, but make do with what you can find—and a cup of scalded milk. You will also need four cups of flour, salt, a pinch of cinnamon, an egg and—this is key—a generous sprinkle of coarsely cut hashish. A handful of currants would not be inappropriate.

When the water has had its way with the yeast, add a soupçon of sugar, cover it up and let it obey its frothy imperative. Cream the butter and the remainder of the sugar, and incorporate the milk. Then, take a few recuperative moments. Enjoy a cup of tea. Smoke a cigarette. When you feel recharged, add the yeast and every remaining ingredient to the butter mixture, setting aside the egg. Knead the dough. Allow it rise.

Now—and this is the fun part—play God. Take your freshly mixed clay and mould it into any shape that pleases you, even your own image. When you are satisfied, break the egg and anoint your cake-to-be with everything it contains. *Voila!* It is ready for the oven. It will take as long as it takes. Golden brown is what you're after.

This All Souls' Cake will make a saint of a sinner and a sinner of a saint. Those of moderate habits, who can lay claim to neither station in life, can be assured of a good sleep and rich dreams. That in itself is something to be grateful for. That alone deserves a deep amen.

LA FONTAINE'S VERSIFIED WALKING TOUR:
A BRIEF PAUSE FOR CLARIFICATION

Attention, please, cats square and hep—
Before we take another step,
May I address a word to those
Who'd rather have their tour in prose;
Who'd rather hear dogs caterwaul
Than hear a cat spout doggerel.
The "just the facts, ma'am" types who balk
When meter rears its head in talk,
Who crave reportage, plain and terse,
Who are, in short, averse to verse,
And think it crude, the death of wit—
I have three words: Get over it.

It's neither prissy nor effete
To measure out one's speech in feet,
Eschewing chewing prose's cud,
If such a penchant's in your blood.
It seems verse schemes like "a-b-a"
Are coded in my DNA.
Congenitally, I'm inclined,
To mine my mind for lines that rhyme.

Does this distract? Then best make tracks,
Best pull the plug, best fade to black.
You're heading out, sir? Fine. Godspeed.
For those remaining, let's proceed.

The question tourists ask the most
Concerns our usage of the post.
Visitors, surprised to see
Epistolary tendencies,
Will always want to have revealed
Why cats trade letters, stamped and sealed.
That answer, easy as they get,
Is: e-mail hasn't reached us yet.
Look! Here's Colette. Her Cheshire grin
Suggests she's swallowed cream or gin.
Her smirk—post coital—plainly tells
That someone's been in pussy's well.

LETTER: COLETTE TO JIM MORRISON

November 7

Sir:

It is not my habit to initiate correspondence with toms, particularly those with whom I have never exchanged so much as a word. Not one word! How can it be that we have never spoken, not even on that night—so recent—when our explosive passion, all those megatons, flattened every barrier between us? My flesh and your flesh, made molten by the blast, were one flesh, our two breaths one breath. Enmeshed, intertwined and tumbling about on my boudoir floor, we must have looked like a fur-wrapped model of the hydrogen atom trembling towards fission. Brutish grunts spilled from us, yes, and eager cries, but nothing that could pass for speech.

What an aberrance, for words have always been my currency, my key, my passport, my shield. Words have paved my every pathway. Words, tightly woven, have been the net I've thrown to capture the world, and with words I have anatomized it. To use words to make sensible the life of the senses: that has been my purpose and mission, and I have done it, I daresay, exceedingly well. So how is it, then, that we two uttered not a single syllable, and yet I feel we shared the one experience for which I would trade every other? Yes, I would give up language itself just to feel so stirred again.

Sir, do you understand what you have done? You have leached to my surface a lode of shamelessness that no one has mined before. Hence, my longing to show you the most entertaining of my tricks: the way I can stand on my head with my hind legs spread, the deft control I have over deeply buried, little-known muscles, the astonishing extension and flexibility of my tongue. Hence, the way I abase myself with this letter.

That I am writing to you now is, I can assure you, highly, highly irregular. Do you believe me? I don't care if you do. If you laugh at my virginal protestations, if you find them quaint, perhaps even detestable, then so be it. My upbringing demands that I offer such declarations of modesty, whether or not they are credited.

"Remember, Colette," Maman never fails to remind me, each and every time she writes, "that to be a Persian is both an uncommon privilege and a tremendous responsibility. Never forget that you, of all cats, are to this city born. Never forget that our motto, 'I, Persian,' anagrams so neatly to 'Parisien.' This is no accident, chérie. When it comes to language, nothing is accidental."

Maman is the sort of self-assured, rather tiresome anachronism for whom 1789 is just another year. She cannot imagine a universe unregulated by rules of precedence that are rooted in pedigree. For her, breeding is everything, and "I, Persian" should be a passe-partout sufficient to the opening of any door, anywhere, anytime. This was the credo with which I was raised, and it was the first certainty I had to jettison upon my arrival in Père-Lachaise. I quickly learned that, while cats of discernible breed are scarce here, those few who can say "I, Siamese," or "I, Burmese" are not accorded a vaunted status commensurate with their rarity. Indeed, quite the opposite. In my first months here I was held up for ridicule because I was so conspicuously cut from Persian cloth; was subjected to the plebeian scorn to which the aristocracy in this land has so often been treated. What's more, I bore the stigma that attaches to every immigrant, for, as you may well know, I am not native to this place.

I was born a kitten of privilege outside these walls, in the city beyond our city, far across Paris, in the distant and very stylish 16th *arrondissement*. Velvet cushions. Satin sheets. Thick cream, as much as I could drink, served up in porcelain dishes of uncommon translucence. I was cuddled and coddled and combed and cosseted, but the whole while I felt as if I were being smothered. Now, I can see that this was because my soul has always been, from the very moment of its forging, better tooled to serve an artist than a queen of leisure. At the time, however, I had no way of articulating this, no basis of experience by which I could isolate the particular reasons for my anxiety. I would sit at the window and stare down at the street below, the rue Benjamin Franklin, and invent elaborate stories, complex romances about other cats and their comings and goings in the great wide world.

And then, early one April afternoon, when spring had finally gained a foothold and when that selfsame window had been opened to admit some of the enticing outside air, a young tom happened by. He was grey and white and tawny. He was brazen, big and brawny. He looked up and saw me. He grinned his rakish grin. He sang:

Come on, baby,
Baby so fine,
Be my baby.
Baby, be mine.

"Colette," cried Maman, "come back! Come back!"

"I'll write!" was all I answered as I shinnied halfway down the drainpipe, then jumped to the pavement and scampered off behind him, bounding along in an easterly direction, away from the setting sun. Léon. That was his name. He was the first of my rogues, my first charming mongrel, and our romance was as brief as it was intense. What befell my swain, just hours after our meeting, was tragic, but almost certainly for the best. It turned out that Léon was fleeing a spot of trouble in the nearby Bois de Boulogne, something to do with a gambling debt. When his creditors began to crank up the heat, he decided to seek sanctuary with some cousins in the Bois de Vincennes, clear across the city.

Had a speeding truck on the rue de Repos, just outside the entrance to Père-Lachaise, not laid him out flatter than a crêpe, I might well have whiled away my days as a gangster's moll. That would most certainly have been fascinating, but I doubt it would have been as satisfying in the long term as the life I have subsequently led, with all its variety and freedom and romance: la vie bohème.

Dear Léon! I shed a tear over his crushed body—I shall never forget the way his eyes were forced from their sockets and hung on two long filaments, like bloody poppies on wilted stalks—then waited, sensibly, for a break in the traffic, crossed the street and entered the gates of the cemetery. I have lived here ever since, and I have been happy. In both this place and in my skin, I feel content and at home, as if I had fallen from a very great height and landed comfortably, safely, squarely, on my four feet.

During my long, eventful and frequently scandalous life upon two legs, I, Colette, paid very close attention to cats and felt with them a profound affinity. It was no surprise to me to learn, once I had slipped into my present flesh, that the feline tongue is a tonal language, with an extraordinary number of subtleties and many deep nuances. Most upright walkers, I daresay, stop thinking about cat talk once they graduate from nursery school and leave behind the repeated bleatings of "Old MacDonald," with its vapid chorus of "a meow meow here and a meow meow there."

It is only when one finds oneself felicitously domiciled as *Felis domesticus* that one realizes how absurdly homocentric is the world of the upright walker. If only they knew the depth and complexity of our vocalizing! Those several dozen words to which the Inuit have famously laid claim for snow pale next to the vocabulary we have devised to express our various states of desire. Rich beyond easy telling is our glottal and ablative suffused nomenclature for hunger in all its lovely guises. For fish, for meat, for cream. For caressing, for licking, for the most penetrating of carnal indulgences.

Here, by way of a short example, is a poem I have latterly written. You may flatter yourself, sir, to think that you were its inspiration, and, in truth, you would not be mistaken. Here, I recount the thrilling circumstances of our meeting and mating, and issue fervent demands that you come, come, come to me. In these plangent pleadings, joyful exclamations and shrill ululations, I compare you variously to the south wind in May, to *la tour Eiffel* at night, to a thundering pneumatic drill and to a slice of liver ripening in the noonday sun of August. I also cast aspersions on other queens who might vie for your attention and make note, in passing and for purposes that are purely folkloric, of a handkerchief, a lily, a plane tree, a thief swinging from the gallows and a horse-drawn hearse:

Phrrrascipzzcmsntxoooooo,
Uiewacvomtttxxmmmmmm.
Yyyyqrepglamtsssuuuuuuu:
Unununununununnnnnnnn.
Mgutrrrrsssbbuumchichichi!
Sssssnnfreeegasssspripripri!
Grrrrrsfzxcvtpwvbrmimimi:
Jysargchr! Nytstsgf! Krrru!

How can I say it plainer? Come to me, Morrison. Come to me soon. No word could ever express my longing, unless that word is hunger.

Yours, and yours only,
C.

✣

ALICE B.

Knowing what I know about the soul and about the strict recycling protocol to which it is a signatory, I have little regard for resurrectionists who claim that the righteous dead will one day pop up from their graves, clothed in incorruptible flesh, as summarily and as cheerily as English muffins out of the toaster. When I cruise the grounds of Père-Lachaise and study the resting arrangements foisted on the deceased by their well-meaning executors, I think this might be just as well. There are many here who, come the Rapture, will wipe the dust from their refurbished eyes, gaze upon their companion of the last hundred years and then keel right over from the shock.

Would Alfred de Musset—long in love with George Sand—necessarily respond with fraternal glee upon finding himself cosied up not with his mistress but rather with his sister? Guillaume Apollinaire and Jacqueline Kolb, who repose here as grave mates, had been married for only a few months before he died, in 1918. I knew them, and from what I recall of their tenuous grasp on domestic accord, I can say with some assurance that the bickering would have begun before they'd spat the earth from their mouths. Of course, there are others who would embrace gladly, remark on how well the other looks and then pick up the conversation exactly where they left off. Gertrude and I would be among that happy crew.

I try to organize my daily rambles so that I pass through the

94th division, which is where we two lie, head to head, like long-stilled propeller blades awaiting a kindly hand that will set us spinning. I made my way there this afternoon, thinking it would be the ideal place to profit from a brief spate of pleasant weather. The stubborn snow was at last no more. Yesterday's lacerating rain had washed away the prayer shawls from the shoulders of the angels and freshened the complexions of all the pretty virgins standing in a row. The sky, so long an unbroken field of grey cloud, had been tilled by the sun.

Content and calm, I settled into a discreet hidey-hole across the avenue Circulaire from the granite block that marks our lying-in spot to enjoy our grave's admirable austerity. The site is fronted by a simple rectangular enclosure, gravel lined and bordered by small boxwoods. The flat top of the stone was peppered, as it always is, with pebbles, placed there in accordance with the Jewish tradition of leaving a stone in remembrance. I studied, as I have many thousands of times before, the carved summation of my Allegheny gal's living and dying, which provides enduring evidence that, however short the text, a good proofreader should always be engaged:

Gertrude Stein Allfghany 3 February 1874—Paris 29 July 1946

There are two significant errors. July 27, not 29, was the day of her passing—I should know, I was there. And Allfghany will never be found in any atlas or gazetteer. I suppose I should be appalled by such carelessness, but, in fact, the chiselled typo only makes me smile. I look forward to showing it to Gertrude. She'll find it amusing, too. Spelling was never her strong suit.

Most days I visit her grave, which is my grave, too, and I remember life as it was and imagine life as it will be. I tend to the tomb alone, but my solitude is never long lived. Today was no exception. Attracted by the approaching murmur of voices, I turned to see two women, arm in arm, ascending the avenue Greffulhe. They paused, looked indecisively one way, then another, consulted their map, consulted one another, achieved consensus, turned east and made their way in my direction. Their ensembles reflected a penchant for practicality rather than couture. Matching anoraks. Sturdy hips contained by denim trousers. Sensible hiking boots. Short-cropped hair, shot through with silver. Glasses, slightly smudged. Rucksacks replete with—I could guess—bottled water, guidebooks, flashlights, cameras, pepper spray.

Such women in such uniforms are not strangers here. I hardly ever come to the 94th without seeing at least one such matched set of vigil keepers. The English, the Germans, the Dutch, the Americans, the Japanese: from all over the world they come to stand before our grave, heads bowed in tribute. Some maintain a meditative silence. Others tell tales. In the dwindling light of the afternoon, I listened with interest to the informed colloquy of the two *touristes du jour*. The things they had to tell! The surviving minutiae never cease to amaze me.

"She couldn't drive in reverse," said one, shaking her head in amazement. "Did you know that?"

"Who?"

"Stein. She was fine when it came to forward, but she was hopeless at backing up."

This is typical of what I hear: the bizarre bits of biographical ballast the living use to weigh down the memory of the dead. Dress and dining, friendships and betrayals, comings and goings: I have heard it all, heard what is real and true, heard half-baked verities. I have heard bald, unalloyed fabrications. Sometimes, I have heard what is hurtful and hateful.

"She was famously ugly."

"Gertrude?"

"Alice. Her moustache was something to behold."

This is often mentioned, and I long ago stopped taking offence. Indeed, I am now unaccountably pleased that, of all the parts that made me, it is my hirsute upper lip they choose to recall.

"I wonder if Gertrude ever cooked."

"I doubt it. I think it was always Alice in the kitchen and Gertrude at her desk, scribbling away, scribbling and scribbling."

"Scribbling and meeting great men. She was lucky she had such an accommodating girl friend."

Girl friend! That rankles. It has such an air of triviality, of impermanence. Gertrude was my husband. I was her wife. This was how we named ourselves. She called me "baby precious." She called me her "dear wifey."

"I think Gertrude took her for granted. Alice, I mean."

"That happens with most couples."

"What?"

"That one takes the other for granted."

"Does it?"

"I think so."

Silence.

"Oh."

This, too, I have often seen before, and I knew very well that they were weighing the mutuality of their affection, analysing who mostly gives and who mostly takes, who mostly cooks and who mostly eats. I knew they were testing their feet against the footprints we two left behind. They were each assessing which of them—within the walls of their private enterprise—was Gertrude? Which was Alice? Perhaps I should find this flattering, but in truth it strikes me as absurd that any extinct firm, even that of Stein and Toklas, should be a template, a yardstick against which other unions are measured. Strange are the ways of the upright living, and never stranger than when they walk among the dead.

The silence went on and on until, at last, one of the women stamped her feet. She shivered.

"Come on, Ginny. Let's go. It's cold. I'm hungry."

"But what about Piaf? What about Colette?"

"Another time."

"Yes. No! Wait!"

"What?"

"I nearly forgot. Turn around."

The one called Ginny pulled off her gloves and held them in her teeth while she unzipped one of the many compartments of her companion's backpack. From it, she extracted a single red rose, somewhat the worse for wear. Deep within her own capacious pockets, Ginny searched for and found a pen and notepad. She scribbled down a few words and ripped out the page. With great reverence, she laid both the flower and her message atop the flat slab, alongside all the pebbles.

"What did you write?"

"Nothing, really. Nothing important."

"Nothing?"

"You'd think it was silly. Anyway, it's cold. Let's go."

"Funny little Ginny," said her friend, with a patronizing chuckle, then wrapped her companion in her arms and bestowed a wet kiss on her brow. They stood there for a minute or more, clinging to each other, an amalgam of subfusc winter wear, while somewhere, deep beneath all that insulation, suspended within the ossified cage of their ribbings, their two hearts sang their secret songs. Then they broke apart. They linked arms and walked away, passing through the Jardin du Souvenir without studying the inscription on the stone's other side:

Alice B. Toklas San Francisco April 30 1877 Paris 7 Mars 1967

I waited until they had been absorbed by the dusk and distance before leaping to the top of the tomb to read Ginny's note. It was exactly what I expected:

"A rose is . . ."

How often have I seen this? Pilgrim after pilgrim enacts this same ritual, and the message never changes:

"A rose is . . ."

It saddens me. How many words did she write, my
Gertrude, how many hundreds of thousands of words, only to
have all her genius reduced to these three syllables, to this
ellipsis? The ranging epic of her days boiled down to a childish game of fill-in-the-blank.

We can never tell how history will treat us. Posterity brooks
no second guessing. Which is preferable? To be forever allied
with a floral koan or with a lavishly endowed upper lip? It is,
I suppose, a distinction to have owned an ugliness that resists
the erosions of time, to be remembered as a kind of anti-
Helen. Not so very much has changed since my whiskers
replaced my moustache. Now, as then, I know that I will never
be named a beauty queen, and the absence of this possibility
does not interfere with my sleep. I could take comfort, if
comfort I required, in knowing that I can always lay claim to
the crown of Queen of Cooking and Good Deeds. I hold, in
perpetuity, the deed to the title of Miss Mitzvah.

"Dear Miss Toklas," they all marvel, as I pass by with my
panniers full of treats, "out and about once again, making her
deliveries. Such a good soul!"

What would they say, I wonder, if they knew the truth? That
I am working for the advancement of my own interests. That I
make my tisket-a-tasket way through the world, benignly dis-
tributing my bits of baking, in order to ingratiate myself and
to ascertain that all systems are go, that every likely path has
been smoothed for the inbound Gertrude. She will come. She
will come. Every sign points in her direction.

"Delicious biscuits, Miss Toklas," said Maria Callas, helping herself to a second and a third. "So light and airy.
Strange, but I can't seem to eat enough these days."

"Lovely pâté, as always, Miss Toklas," smiled Colette.
"Mercy, but I'm peckish!"

"Don't tempt me, Miss Toklas," sighed Isadora Duncan,
when I offered her a plate of profiteroles. "I really shouldn't,
but if you insist—"

Uncommon hunger: a sure symptom that my great plan is

evolving as I intended. As I have no way of knowing which of these queens harbours the Good Ship Gertrude, I must be more vigilant than ever and determined in my intelligence-gathering. I look to each day's post with a renewed sense of urgency.

"My poor feet!" Tristesse whines, each and every noon when she comes home for lunch, her bag still bulging with undelivered mail.

"Have a little nap before you head back out," I tell her, and she needs no encouraging. Directly she's asleep, I sift through her mailbag, open and read the most promising or threatening of its passengers. Some I carefully reseal and send on their way. Others—when they contain information or instructions, codes or procedures, that are inimical to my needs—I consign to the flames. Up and up and up they go, all those pages, all those words. Up and up and up, from my fire to God's ear. News translated into smoke. Chatter into cinders.

Today, for example, I was able to disrupt the destructive scheming of the good old toms network. Baron Haussmann, not content with having run roughshod over Paris when he stalked the world on two legs, is determined to effect the same changes in the necropolis that is Père-Lachaise. Here is a page from his letter to Baron Rothschild:

Dear Rothsy:

Good to have seen you at the Renaissance Club this afternoon. You're looking very well, to say nothing of prosperous! I wanted to follow up our conversation with a short note, as you expressed a more than casual interest in my redevelopment scheme. One only has to whisper the word "demolition" in this hidebound purlieu to set the fur flying. There is no doubt that our biggest challenge will be the preservationists, who manage simultaneously to be both deeply conservative and highly emotional.

Cats! Why is it that they are so opposed to anything that resembles reason? Why are so many wedded to the place they know and so attached to the merely familiar that they cannot entertain the possibility—however clearly it is articulated—that there might be a better way? I am not like that, Rothsy, and nor are you, I daresay. Good Lord!

All these twisty alleys that lead nowhere, these minor paths that peter out before they've properly begun! Instinct is all well and good, and spirals have their place, but when it comes to actually tracking down an address, nothing beats a good old reliable grid system. But try telling that to the likes of Miss Toklas and see what you get! A snippy little lecture about the imposition of a phallic imperative, whatever the hell that means.

Truly, Rothsy! How can they not see that this hodgepodge of ziggurat and menhir, obelisk and basilica, pyramid and sepulchre, is a gross offence to the eye? How can they not see that their interests, both practical and aesthetic, would be better served by a single and singular vision that could bring to Père-Lachaise a homogeneity of design, a marriage of form and function?

There are ways to do it, Rothsy. I have made inquiries, and some very interesting combustibles are available through certain black market connections. And now that we seem to be on the verge of a population explosion—at least, this is the word that reaches me from usually reliable sources—the time is ripe to begin propagandizing in earnest. We need merely put it about, in a persuasive way, that a revamped Père-Lachaise would be a better deal for all the coming kitties, which will surely attract the support of—

At which point, I had read enough, and the rant became fodder for the flame. Haussmann! A windy bore, and so risibly easy to manage. Tomorrow, I'll send him some of my famous fudge, an especially potent batch, and he'll soon be content to build his stately pleasure domes out of air, and of this I shall be glad. Arisen is arisen is arisen, and when Gertrude comes, she will find this place—these sacred groves, these verdant acres of the dead—exactly as they are and have always been. Which is exactly how they will remain, always, as long as I have my strength of will. As long as I have a pan to bake in.

⚜

La Fontaine's Versified Walking Tour: Isadora Duncan

It always seems to happen, friends,
As past these tombs one slowly wends,
A certain *gravitas* descends:
A mood of melancholy.
Inevitably, graveyards spawn
The fear that when we're dead and gone
We'll never see another dawn.
But that's the food of folly,
Snack not thereon! Instead, be wise,
Just look around, believe your eyes.
The buried do not claim the prize
Of lulled, sepulchral boredom.
One lapses, then one goes to seed,
But soon one howls, and soon one breeds.
In other words, the life one leads
Is full, not dull, post mortem.

It's radical, of course, that shift
From man to cat. The corporal rift
Is easier to breach when gifts
From life to life are lifted.
For instance, when I was a man,
I spoke in rhyme, and still I can.
Is this how one defines CAT scan?
(That couldn't be resisted!)
Now, here's another case in point,
Or rather, should I say, *en pointe*.
This lithesome creature I'd anoint
As Terpsichore's fair daughter.
It's Isadora, all bedight
With ribbons, whirling through the night.
In this life, too, she's air, she's light,
She's earth, she's fire, she's water.

⚜

Isadora, bedight with ribbons

LETTER: ISADORA DUNCAN TO MODIGLIANI

November 10

Dearest Modi:

Remember the way you turned up the other night with that come-hither look in your eye and that eager question on your lips? "Wanna ride my train?" was what you asked, and I got on. Remember the way you huffed and puffed? The way you kept repeating, "I think I can, I think I can"? Remember how you yelled "All aboard!" at the very second you discharged all those happy passengers? You'll never guess what's happened now. It looks like those travellers booked a berth for the next two months. Do you follow, Modi? Do you hear what I'm telling you? There's a full moon on the rise. There are groceries in the sack. The burger is fully loaded. I'm preggers, Modi.

Are you happy? Impressed? Distressed? All of the above? As for me, I can't say I'm surprised. In fact, I knew it was happening, right at the moment of impact. I knew while you were still lying on top of me, with your teeth sunk into my neck and your hot breath in my ear. When you're a dancer, you learn how to read your body like a map pinned to the wall. You learn to interpret its every shift and contour. You know its shapes and borders so well that any little change registers. And what I'm trying to say is that, the second you let fly, I felt it. I mean I felt that cleaving. I felt my future change. I felt my teats begin to swell. That was just a few days ago, and now none of my geography is the same.

Do you think I'm flaky, Modi? Callas does. I told her what I've just told you, and she said, "That's the problem with dancing, Isadora. All that jouncing of the cerebellum in its pan. Some vital cortex gets bruised. You lose touch with reality. You start imagining things." Like she should talk! Every time she hits a high C, I think she kills off some more brain cells. What's more, I'd be willing to bet that she's knocked up, too. She had that telltale smirk on her clock, that well-oiled

"I-just-got-serviced" look, and I detect a certain roundness to her hips that wasn't there before. All the signs are there that someone's been diving on the diva.

But all of this is beside the point. I'm telling you this because you might want to know. I'm not trying to rope you into anything, not trying to fence you in. I'm not big on fences myself, as you know. I'm a free spirit, Modi, just like you. So, I'll have these kittens and then move on.

One other thing, Modi. It's a little strange. I had a letter from Miss Toklas today:

Dear Miss Duncan:

I hope both that this finds you well and that you will excuse the intrusion. I am writing to put to you a proposition which I hope you might find worthy of welcome. You must know that I have been waiting for my friend Miss Stein to come to Père-Lachaise for quite some time now. In anticipation of her imminent arrival—and I have every reason to believe she will be here soon—I am endeavouring to make a few changes to my house, in order that she feel at home here. Miss Stein was, in her two-legged days, a discerning and tireless collector of Art, so I have decided to commission a portrait or two to hang on the walls of our abode on the rue Anglais. Would you be good enough, Miss Duncan, to sit for such an undertaking?

Perhaps this will strike you as an odd, even an invasive request, but I do hope you won't dismiss it out of hand. I am asking you not only because you are comely—and heaven knows that would be reason enough—but also because I want to provide a demonstration of continuum, which I believe Miss Stein will find helpful in the liminal phase through which we must all pass when first we arrive, as translations. I do not know you well enough, Miss Duncan, to be able to guess whether or not you have retained any detailed memory of your life as an upright walker. If you have not, you may be interested to learn that, when you were a child, you were a neighbour of Miss Stein's, in far-off California. Indeed, you stole apples from her father's orchard! I think it would give Miss Stein a rosy feeling about the future if she could see the proof that remnants of her past still linger in the present.

As to the artist, I know that you circulate in a particular milieu and that you have connections with any number of painters. If there is one with whom you

*feel a particular sympathy and to whom you would care to entrust your immor-
talization, I am happy to take your advice. I can't offer you riches, but I promise to feed both you and your portraitist well.*

*Thank you, Miss Duncan. I look forward to hearing from you and to seeing
you soon.*

Yours very truly,
A.B.T.

So, Modi. What do you figure? Is she loco? I'm starting to
think so. Miss Stein this, Miss Stein that, Miss Stein round
the maypole. Miss Toklas has always been loopy, but it's getting worse. I think we should have paid attention when she
threw herself at Ondine all those years ago. I think it was cry
for help. And now this. A portrait! Oh, well. There's nothing wrong with her cooking, that's for sure. And these days,
I'm so hungry I'm sure that I must be eating for eight.

What do you say, Modi? Do you feel like having your way
with me again? This time with paints? You could paint me
thin and dancing, wrapped around with ribbons. You could
paint me big and round, my belly dragging on the ground.
You could give me a long, thin neck. That would be something you could sink your teeth into. Would you, Modi? Do
say yes. Answer soonest.

I am,
your Isadora

⚜

ALICE B.

I will describe where we live, Tristesse and I, which is where
Gertrude will live, too, my wandering husband. My absent
Elijah. Every night I set a place for her, and every night I
pray that no well-meaning hand will smear the lintel with
the blood of the lamb; for she is my angel, and I would die

to know that she had come and seen and passed me over. The flame that flickers behind the iron grille of my one small window may draw any number of visitors, but it is for her and her alone that I keep it lit. Every night I light my lamp—there is no shortage of candles hereabout, as you may imagine—and listen patiently for her insistent knock, her willing tread. I will know them when I hear them, just as I know she will know that this is the house I am keeping for her, even though it is not her name, nor mine, chiselled above the door: *Laporte*, it says. Also inscribed there is the slogan so widely posted in these environs: *Concession à perpétuité.* That is, this is mine forever.

Promenade down any of the stony paths and byways of this wide precinct—the chemin Beaujour, the chemin des Dragons, the chemin des Chèvres—and everywhere you will see that same vain proprietary claim affixed to family memorials at the behest of ancients long gone to dust. No doubt, in the drawn-out days of their final withering, they found comfort in the absurdly optimistic certainty that their dynasties would endure, that they would go on and on, from generation unto generation, forever and ever, amen.

Concession à perpétuité. Reserved for all eternity. Ha! If only they could see how their vanity has been repaid. If only they knew how many of their lavish graves are left unattended, their ornate granite or limestone shrines consigned to the predations of the elements, the tourists, the addicts, the trysting lovers. Locks have been broken. Doors fit for bank vaults now swivel open, registering every passing breeze. Sarcophagi have been unsealed and looted, stained-glass windows smashed to smithereens.

Our own sweet home was, once upon a time, the fetid embodiment of just such neglect. The clan Laporte might well have staked its everlasting claim to our cottage, but it has been many years since anyone called Laporte darkened the door. When I took the place over, its interior was a rank collage of bottles and shards, piss-soaked rags and ends of fags, syringes of dubious sterility and a midden-like heap of contraceptive casings. As soon as Oscar got wind of my plans, he scuttled by to take a gander.

"Oh, my dear," he sighed, recoiling at the sight of the mouldering excrescence and the pungent wafts of rotting detritus, "tell me it isn't so."

"Don't be deceived by surfaces, Oscar. After all, beauty is only skin deep."

"Never disparage a surface. Nothing recommends beauty more than its superficiality. Real beauty walks through the world uncluttered and unmasked. It doesn't hide in the earth like a truffle, attendant on the tender mercies of a passing pig."

"It needs some work, as anyone can see. But it has great potential."

" 'Great potential' is a phrase used only by short-sighted parole officers and cunning real estate agents."

I squared the shoulders of my first resolve. The deed was done and there was nowhere to go but on. If I had strapped myself to the back of a white elephant, so be it. Let it rampage. I would hang on for dear life and never look back.

"I like it, Oscar. That's all there is to say about it."

"There are more pleasurable ways of courting punishment, if punishment is what you're after. There's a club I know, a low dive not far from here—"

"Don't be louche. This will suit me very well. Suit *us*, I mean. Tristesse and I for the time being, Gertrude when she comes."

"But will she stay when she sees the digs?"

"The digs will clean."

"Seven maids with seven shovels couldn't make a dent in these digs."

"Tristesse will help."

"*Toujours* Tristesse, of course. Always looking for a way to live down to her name."

"She is my sister, Oscar."

Tristesse, trailing Oscar

"And blood is dimmer than water."

"Come back in a week, Oscar, and you'll see. I'll give you something to eat, other than your words."

All that was years ago. Now, my candle glows in the window. There are flowers on the table. Our house may be wee, but abundance abounds; for the moon is full and the larder is full and my heart is full. Only the bed is empty: half empty, rather, and that, I can tell you, is sadder than a wholesale vacancy.

"Well," sniffed Oscar, grudgingly, when a week had passed and he came to gloat, "perhaps you were right. It's not without possibilities." He helped himself to the snack Tristesse had prepared and silently served: rice crackers smeared liberally with Gentleman's Relish. This was the tenth time she had passed him the plate. And yes, I was counting.

Tristesse is always very solicitous of Oscar when he comes to call. Her importunate ways bespeak an affection that is not, I fear, mere friendship. I have tried to dissuade her from investing anything like hope in the prospect of Oscar, but her only response to my counsel is a look of dumb confusion.

"Yes," he said, surveying my progress, "I can see that you may have been right about the potential. It's small, and there's nothing to be done about that. But it has good bones."

"Irony intended?"

"There's not a drop in me. I have irony-poor blood. Thank you, Tristesse, I will have another. They're delicious. Tell me, Miss Toklas, where do you find such comestibles as these? Scrumptious. Just scrumptious."

"I have my ways and sources."

"Sphinx! I love the way you lower your eyes to half-mast when you've got a little secret. If you weren't promised to another, I would have you for my own."

Which made Tristesse wince and made me bite my tongue to contain my laughter. I have seen what Oscar takes for his own, and believe me, hors d'oeuvres are the only wares I have on offer that he would see fit to taste. From that day to this, he has continued to frequent our house of good bones. Many visitors beat a path to my door, and little wonder. Whether one walks through the world on two legs or four, food and opiates are a considerable lure. All I ask in exchange for my hospitality is the pleasure of their company and the diversion of their stories. All I ask is that they help me kill time, for it is only time that stands in the way of my reunion with Gertrude.I take their words and I fasten them to my loom. I weave them into the fabric I spread before you here. They are my blanket, my cloak. This is what keeps me warm while I wait for my love, my puss. My lost Ulysses, buffeted by winds and racked by storms, but coming, coming, coming from afar, unswervingly and ineluctably coming and coming towards me.

LA FONTAINE'S VERSIFIED WALKING TOUR: MARIA CALLAS

When Death decides it's come your turn,
You have to opt for earth or urn.
Maria Callas, when she died,
Said no to "buried," yes to "fried";
No casket grand with brassy hinge,
It's over when the singer's singed.
Her loved ones came to pick her up,
They took Maria—half a cup—
And housed her, feeling rather glum,
Within the columbarium.

Soon, student pranksters, on a spree,
Connived to set Maria free.
They planned the heist, they named the day,
They stole the ash, then stole away.

A gendarme, acting on a tip,
Restored the cinders to the crypt.
Maria's kin, inclined to nix
All future sophomoric tricks,
Yanked the rug from young collegians,
Scattered her on the Aegean.

In her blue, refulgent cloister,
La Divina feeds the oysters.
Free of ballast, safe from malice,
Au revoir, Maria Callas.
That is, goodbye to human flesh:
A cat skin is her soul's new cache.
She's black and white and grey and tan,
And oh, the voice! "Sing!" plead her fans.
They beg in vain, in vain beseech,
For divas e'er stay out of reach.

INTERVIEW: MARIA CALLAS SENDS A FORM LETTER

November 12

To Whom It May Concern:
I am in receipt of your letter dated _____ requesting an
interview for your ( )magazine ( )newspaper ( )website ( )radio
show ( )television program. While I am grateful for your
interest in my career, I fear I must decline your kind invita-
tion. Life is simply too short. In the few lines that follow, you
will find every answer to every question I would willingly have
entertained had a face-to-face encounter been possible. You
have my express permission to use this in whole or in part, to
represent it as your original work and to attach to it your by-
line, without fear of calumny or reprisal from this quarter.

M.C.

Q: *Madame Callas, what was your reaction when you discovered that you had been reborn as a cat?*

A: Initially, surprise, of course. Why would one expect otherwise? It is nothing one would think to ask for, after all, and then so much is so vastly different from what one has previously known. Perspective. Instinct. Longing. The sudden urge to hold one's foot to one's mouth and suck on it, and the easy flexibility that makes such carnal indulgences a possibility. It's all quite unanticipated, as you can readily imagine. However, astonishment soon gives way to willing acquiescence. And why would it not? If there's one thing one learns from a life in the opera, it's that destiny will not be denied.

When the Fates have you in their sights, you may just as well open your arms wide in a gesture of welcoming embrace and make yourself a conspicuous target. Concealment is useless, for they are relentless; the Fates, I mean. Eventually, they will track you down. When you accept that this is your lot and that this is the hand you have been dealt, you require neither explanation nor consolation. You merely accede to the fact that this life, like any other, is nothing more or less than a costume party: *un ballo in maschera*, as Verdi would have it. Did you ever see my Amalia, by the way? I can recommend my 1957 La Scala performance, Gianandrea Gavazzeni conducting.

Q: *I know that recording. I adore it.*

A: Of course you do. Who could cavil at perfection?

Q: *Do I understand that you have no regrets about your present situation?*

A: None. *Je ne regrette rien.*

Q: *I take it that you are acquainted with Madame Piaf?*

A: Everyone knows Edith. She's the most sought-after laundress in Père-Lachaise. Her mangling is above reproach.

Q: *She cleans rather than sings?*

A: Her art, like my own, was as much incantatory as it was musical. Her true talent, in that other place, that other time, was to cut through the dross, the encumbrances, to reveal to her audience the unsullied heart of matter. In other words, she was endowed with the ability to cleanse and make pure. She still is. Her gift remains intact. All that has changed is the medium of its delivery. In her singing days, she used her voice to reverse the flow of blood from the head to the heart. Now that she has come to live at Père-Lachaise, she knows how to reverse the effects of bloodstains on sheets. Both skills are priceless, and they grow from the same root.

Q: *Do you often have blood on your sheets?*

A: Young man, that is a foolish question coming from someone who claims to know about opera. Does the word "tubercular" mean nothing to you? Have you any idea how many consumptive heroines I have had thrust upon me? How many Violettas I have had to wrestle to the ground? Bloodstained sheets are the least of it.

Q: *So, unlike Piaf, you continue to sing.*

A: I could not do otherwise.

Q: *Are there roles that are particularly well-suited to your present circumstances?*

A: Tosca, most especially. I can throw myself from the parapet and land on my feet without risk of injury. And then the audience is always mightily impressed when I leap right back up again for an encore. Up and down, up and down. Why, I could go up and down all night and hardly break a sweat.

Q: *So rumour has it. Would you care to comment on reports linking you romantically to Mr. Morrison?*

A: Ha! Why not just come right out and ask if I'm bearing his love child? One hears that, too! From what polluted well are these lunatic speculations drawn? The only way to deal with such excremental musings is to bury them in the sand. Which now I do. There. See? They are gone.

Q: *Nonetheless, several reliable sources report seeing Mr. Morrison with his teeth sunk deeply into your neck.*

A: Quite. Mr. Morrison, who is skilled in first aid, was assisting me to remove a small fishbone that had become lodged in my craw. I am fortunate he happened to be passing by at just that moment. Otherwise, surgery would surely have been required. Who knows what deleterious effect a tracheotomy would have had on my instrument? Mr. Morrison was most generous and most efficient. His was a very welcome interference.

Q: *Still, it must have been painful. Every report has it that you were howling.*

A: Young man, that was not howling. That was my Salome.

Q: *I do beg your pardon.*

A: As well you might. Are we done now?

Q: *Nearly. Latterly, many operatic singers have been forging collaborations with pop stars. Do you think that you and Mr. Morrison might undertake such a partnership?*

A: Oh, my goodness! Can you imagine Mr. Morrison singing "E Lucevan Le Stelle"?

Q: *It would be sauce for the gander after your recent performance of "Come on Baby, Light My Fire," would it not?*

A: Why, look at that clock. I believe it is time for you to go. Goodbye, young man.

Q: *But—*

A: Young man, goodbye.

⚜

HANDBILL DELIVERED TO ALL HOMES

Announcing Auditions for
THE ANNUAL RENAISSANCE REVUE

Auditions will be held on Sunday for the annual Père-Lachaise Renaissance Revue.

The revue will take place on Christmas Eve in the Columbarium Theatre.

We are looking for solo performers, as well as mime participants for the tableau vivant portion of the evening.

Actors, dancers and instrumentalists should be prepared to present a brief rendition of their work: no longer than three minutes, please.

All singers are required to perform one of two test pieces, the queen or the tom version, kindly composed for us this year by Georges Bizet.

We look forward to seeing you Sunday!

Test Piece for Toms

(Bizet —Toreador)

Tom cats of Pa - ris,   strong and stiff and   proud_   Out on the   prowl_

Rea - dy to howl_   We're   at your ser - vice   ma'am we'll waste no   time._

All   our   can - nons are   primed._____   We're_   ea - ger and we're preened

We're_   fair - ly   clean___   We're   here to   serve   our

queen.   Tom - cats, tom - cats on   the prowl   Tom - cats, tom - cats set   to

howl_____   Yes,   real -   ly   howl._____

Test Piece for Queens

(Bizet —Habanera)

Allegretto quasi andantino

When your pri-vates be-come en-gorged, When worms of want - ing in-fest your

tripes, When your long-ings are su - per-charged, It's then you know that the time is

ripe. When a ting-ling has seized your thighs, When ev-'ry tom__ smells like rea-dy

meat, When you'd gouge out your best friend's eyes, It's then you know that your in-to

espress.

heat.__ Meow meow meow meow meow meow

_p_

meow meow When you're in heat, Each tom's a toy, You long for no-thing but a-chiev-ing

bliss, And when you meet That bump-tious boy, You know you're des-tined to do more than

kiss.__ Each tom's a toy, A play-thing rea-dy for you night and day.__

And best of all Is, when it's o - ver he'll just go a - way!__

LA FONTAINE'S VERSIFIED WALKING TOUR: EDITH PIAF

Some cats are eager optimists,
They see *la vie en rose*.
Madame Piaf, I'm bound to say,
Would not be one of those.
If she possessed a stylish flat
Or château on the Loire,
She'd nonetheless be unimpressed
And see *la vie en noir*.

She welcomes in catastrophe,
She notes each danger sign.
Malignancy's what she expects,
Instead of bland benign.
She's off to see Miss Toklas now,
Who's whipping up a stew,
With brownies for dessert! She'll have
Her cake and Edith, too.

ALICE B.

Today my mother came to call, as she reliably does each and every Wednesday afternoon. Do you imagine a sweet old thing, perhaps a little forgetful, perhaps a little shaky on her feet, who arrives in a cloud of lavender scent, bestows on her cherished daughter fond kisses, one on each cheek, and then sits to enjoy a cosy tête-à-tête and the genial sharing of inter-generational confidences over a cup of steaming tea and a plate of crispy biscuits? That's not the way it goes.

Instead, Piaf turns up at the door with her bleach and her mangle, hammers twice before entering of her own accord, then launches without preamble into the honing of her triple vocations: laundering, complaining and gossiping. She is a very able monologist, and I do not think that we have ever had the kind of back and forth that might pass for a conversation. Indeed, we have neither of us ever acknowledged our blood connection. What would be the point?

For Piaf, motherhood was only the by-product of her role as desire's willing plaything. Her pandering to base biology was never mitigated by anything maternal or nurturing. It would seem unnatural to call Edith "Mother," and I feel no more lovingly connected to her than I might to a toll booth through which I was once obliged to pass. I am quite certain she has no recollection whatsoever that, once upon a time, I clawed my way out of her womb. Why would she? Piaf produced litters of kittens with such unseemly rapidity that she could no more remember them than a Gatling gun could keep track of its fallen shell casings.

In any case, the time of her rampant fertility is long past. She no longer exudes the pheromonal waft that once kept her dance card full. Nature has removed her from that market, thank God. Now, she channels all her sour energy into her work. There is nothing Edith loves more than the airing of dirty laundry, both literally and figuratively. She studies sheets and pronounces on the stains like an Old Testament prophet scanning a spill of sheep gut. Then she goes out into the world and merrily imparts the news of whatever she has divined to all and sundry. Rumour is to Edith what the plague is to a rat, and as I am forever on the lookout for any news of Gertrude's impending arrival, I now pay close attention to my mother as she mongers scandals while she mangles towels. Here is the rude distillation of this afternoon's crude harangue.

"What have you got for me today? Tablecloths again? Yeah, I should have guessed. It's always tablecloths for Miss Toklas. How many, then? One, two, three, four. Jesus, girl! Four! Here then, what's this? Gravy? Christ almighty! You might just as well pass me the scissors, cutting's the only way to get this out. No, no, never mind, I'll do my best. No promises, though. No promises.

"Any sign of that Miss Stein yet? The one you're always on about? No? Hell, girl, you've been waiting a long time, ain't ya? I never did figure what makes her so goddamn special. She wrote books, you told me that, but so what? I never could understand why anyone would want to do such a thing. It's not as if there aren't enough books already, more than anyone could ever read, and as near as I can see, most of 'em are crap. I mean, writing! Jesus! Why would anyone do it? All that time alone, sitting and staring. Why not just lock yourself in a closet and try to force blood out of your ears?

"Jesus, Miss Toklas! This gravy! What do you put in it? Blood? You do? Well, no wonder! Where was I? Oh, yeah. Books. Hell, I could write a book. The things I see! It'd be a damn sight easier than laundering, that's for sure. I'm getting too old for this, but what the hell else am I going to do? Kitten-sit? There'll soon be a market for that, I can tell you. Too bad I can't stand little brats. That Sarah Bernhardt. She might be missing a leg, but someone's been giving her the old leg over, you can bet. And have you seen Colette? Big as a house already! She's going to have a job teaching those yoga classes of hers, I can tell you. As for Callas, she can go on pretending as much as she wants that she's spent her whole life holding an aspirin between her knees. Someone got to her, for sure, and I think I know who. The three-balled wonder. There's no stopping him. He gets to everyone eventually. Christ knows I had him more times than I could count.

"Yeah, like I was saying, I'm getting too old for this. No one appreciates you, they dump all over you every chance they get. Like that Bonne Maman bitch. Did I tell you what happened? I was over there the other day, scrubbing away at her filthy old skivvies, and she comes up to me and starts asking if I'd moved some of her books, she was missing some special book. She asked in a way that very accusing, you know what I'm saying, and I didn't appreciate it one bit. I said, 'I don't give a cold piss about your goddamn book, so screw off,' which she did. She knows I won't take crap from her, I don't care if she is a witch.

"Yeah, it's a pain in the arse, this work I do, but I guess I'll keep at it for a while, anyway. Hey, maybe when I die, they'll put up a big old stone for me. They could carve a poem on it, too. Like maybe: 'Always rude and indiscreet / But she could sure clean shit from sheets.' What do you think, Miss Toklas? Would your Miss Stein like that poem? I wrote it myself. Pretty good, eh? Pretty damn good. Nothing to regret there. Nope. Nothing at all.

"There. Look. See? Your tablecloths are done. And so am I. Have you got my fudge? Did you make it strong? Ah, you're a good girl."

And then Piaf was gone, as I must be too. Gone to bed to dream of Gertrude, my one and only, my pristine love.

La Fontaine's Versified Walking Tour: Marcel Proust

You know the kind of cat, perhaps,
Who only lives, it seems, to nap.
Impersonator of the dead,
He lies recumbent on his bed;
Prostrate in a state of wilt,
He never deigns to quit his quilt.
His raison d'être is to roost,
And such a cat is Marcel Proust.
Inert, exempt from drive or torque,
He lies within his room of cork.
With curtains drawn, all pale and wan,
He tries to capture times long gone.

But when Proust tires of chasing time,
He turns his mind to solving crimes.
With nose to tail, he somehow sees
The heart and all its mysteries.

The wide world he'll investigate,
The while his butt he contemplates.
He seldom ever leaves his room
To stalk among the crypts and tombs
But still intuits, from his den,
Who did what to whom and when.
Who and where; what, when and why:
Meet Marcel Proust, the great P.I.

PROUST QUESTIONNAIRE: ONE

Q: How did you become a private investigator?

A: For the longest time I went to bed early. That longest time
was a long time ago, but that time will never be lost to me nor
live outside the possibility of capture, not as long as my spine
retains its miraculous elasticity, its willing pliancy; for as long
as I am able to touch nose to tail and breathe in the heady
perfumes of my own nether quarters, I can be assured that
the walls of time's fortress will crumble into dust, without
benefit even of rams' horns, and that the phalanxes of foot
soldiers conscripted into the past's teeming legions will spill
forth, like Greeks from the hollow belly of their cunning
horse, but with open arms, intent not on conquering but on
embracing the present moment, so that the chasm between
then and now, between kitten and tom, will again be
breached, and I will inhabit—not only in fantasy but in the
hard-coin realm of the literal—those days when bed, just bed,
was the sole object, the focus of all my desire.

I need only place nose to tail, need only suck in the signature wafts, the touchstone whiffs of my own hindmost
parts—that satisfactory olfactory braiding of cheese with clay—
to remember the mewling days of long ago, when the hours

of waking dug in their talons with such raptor-like rapacity that I feared my untempered flesh would never be free of their barbs, that waking would be my anchor and that I would be forever exiled from the country whose soil I longed to kiss, the Republic of Slumber. Then I would grow tearful and run to Maman to beg her reassurance that the sweet surcease of sleep, of dream, would truly come again; and not only sleep and dream but most especially the necessary prelude to their harmonious duet, which was Maman's adoring kiss, without the conferring of which I might just as well have had my heavy lids sutured open; might just as well have been a statue whose wide and staring eyes never knew the bliss of shuttered concealment.

Then, in those long-ago days—before the bestowing of Maman's kiss, but after she had delivered herself of the banshee-banishing blandishments I never tired of hearing; before she leaned down to touch her tongue to my fur, after which caress she would whisper a final "Good night" and leave me to the tender mercies of whatever dreams waited in the wings—then I would beg her to indulge me in a childish sport. She would always comply, though heaven knows it must have been with many an inner sigh, for the script of our play was as fixed and sacred a monument as the Mass.

"Guess, Maman," I would demand as I angled my body into a position commodious for sleep, "guess which pastry I am meant to be!"

"Dear little one," she would answer, without fail, her voice never betraying weariness or reluctance to engage in so fatuous a sport, "are you perhaps a brioche?"

"No!"

"Might you be a napoleon?"

"No!"

"A mille feuille? Tarte tatin? Gâteau St. Honoré?"

"No!"

"A madeleine?"

"No and no and no!" I would trill, in a voice ever more

shrill, until, finally, she would shrug in mock desperation, like the miller's daughter trying to divine the name of Rumplestiltskin, and I would ask if she gave in, and she would wave her small white handkerchief as a sign of surrender.

"A croissant, Maman! I'm a croissant!"

"Of course," she would answer. "Of course you are! How could I not have known? A buttery, warm croissant, to be sure, and good enough to eat, I'd wager!"

Then would come the kiss I craved, and her fond good night. And then, in the settling silence, I would lie with nose to tail—so much like the quarter moon that anyone seeing me quickly and from the corner of an eye might well have thought me a croissant—enjoying the smell that was my very own smell and wondering, as the young will do while waiting for sleep and dream to keep their lofty promises, about the future: wondering especially about what I might become, vocationally, when the day dawned that a career choice became a necessity. Not surprisingly, given that every evening I fancied myself an airy breakfast roll, I fantasized for the longest while that I might one day become a baker or pastry chef; and I might have supplied that imagining with more substance had Maman not told me how early in the day such journeymen are obliged to rise, which prospect made me feel quite ill.

Then, as I derived so much pleasure from the sight of my own posterior crevice, and as I revelled so in the sound of my own pulse and the pleasurable rush of blood through my veins, I wondered if I might not be cut out to be a physician. This plan Maman scotched when she pointed out that such an undertaking would require frequent dousing in blood foreign to my own arteries and close proximity to anterior apertures other than my own, cavities that might well not be quite so pleasingly perfumed, which prospect robbed me of my breath and rendered my knees quite gelatinous.

So it was that every night, while waiting for sleep to take my hand and usher me into the gilded court of dreaming, I would lie, nose to tail, absorbing and savouring my own essence. And likewise every morning—before I opened my eyes but when wakefulness was nevertheless upon me and I was fully steeped in the knowing that, because of some unfathomable offence, I had been yet again turned away from the paradise of temporary oblivion—I would apply myself to trying to solve the delightfully complex riddle of my own being, seeking, always seeking, to discern the ins, the outs, the ups, the downs, the ontological whys and wherefores of the hydra-headed self.

Time passed.

Before I knew it, I was grown, and by then analysis had become so rooted a habit, consolation and need that, *faute de mieux*, my obsession became my profession, and I began, in earnest, my private investigations, my disciplined and rigorous analysis of all that is interior. I hung up my shingle, "Marcel Proust, P.I." and inscribed beneath it the motto of my firm, "In one heart, a universe."

There are those, I know, who wonder how a cat who is so resolute a recluse and so reluctant to leave the confines of his own room can properly unravel the twisted skein of a murder or theft or abduction. How he can deduce a motive or method without ever visiting the scene of the crime, without resorting to the elaborate farrago of forensics on which so many of his colleagues rely? I can answer only that such is not Proust's way. Proust looks no farther than the shady grove of his own heart, needs only to sweep its several dark and secret chambers to ferret out all that is hidden and needful of revelation, wherever and however it lives.

Père-Lachaise has never been a place prone to crime waves; indeed, I cannot remember a time when there was so much as a ripple. But this morning, at 10:27 A.M., came an urgent hammering at my door and the clamorous cry of someone in deep distress.

"Hey! Wake up in there you butt-sniffing sod! Wake up and come to the goddamn door!"

I squinnied through the judas and took note of the sorceress, Bonne Maman, pacing up and down, her hair a static cloud, her eyes half-fried with high-voltage agitation. I braced myself for the onslaught of fresh air, then slid back the grille a crack and listened to her story, just as a priest might hear a confession. In essence, her tale was simple, but it was rendered rather more baroque than necessary by her many colourful remarks pertaining to the terrible vengeance she planned to exact upon the thief who had violated her sanctuary, rifled through her belongings and made off with a book. That is what all this boils down to: a book.

"What sort of book?"

"Spells. Incantations. Formulae."

"Pertaining to?"

"Love."

"Awakening love? Sustaining love? Revitalizing love? Getting rid of love?"

"All of the above."

"When did you last see this book?"

"Round about Halloween."

"You're sure you haven't misplaced it?"

"No, goddamn it! It's gone. Stolen."

"Ah."

"Can you help?"

"I can try."

"How long?"

"I'll get back to you."

Here are the facts. A book is missing. A book of spells. Someone has taken it. Somewhere, in the 114 acres of Père-Lachaise, is a cat who feels a certain desperation about his or her love life. That certainly narrows things down.

Time to proceed. I hold the book in my head. I hold my nose to my rear. I inhale. I listen to my heart. *Go deep*, it says. *Go deep. Go deep.* And so I will. And so begins my investigation.

⚜

LETTER: OSCAR WILDE TO JIM MORRISON

November 15

Dear Heart:

I happened to be passing through the 8th division today and I saw you in the distance, cock of the walk on the chemin du Coq. God's beard! How good you looked as you swaggered along. Have I told you before how beautifully you swagger? It is a rare commodity, these days, a really convincing swagger. It is a souvenir of a less straitened time, of an epoch that was more romantic, more freewheeling, more muscular, more—dare I say it?—manly. You are swaggering's last hope and refuge, Jamz. Long may you strut.

I followed behind at a discreet distance, stopping now and again to sniff where you had sprayed. Ambrosia! The day was grey and punctuated by pockets of mist. Sometimes the hungry fog would swallow you, and I would redouble my pace so as not to lose sight of your marvellous machinery: the stiff shaft of your tail, the driving pistons of your haunches, the confident swing of those three ball bearings. Happy the day that nature, through either whimsy or accidental misallotment, crafted so divine a trinity! Three big balls, hanging 'twixt tail and haunch, like the globes outside the pawnshop where you keep my heart in hock. And mine, it seems, is not the only heart gathering dust on its groaning shelves.

"Magnificent, isn't he?"

A husky voice shattered my ambulatory reverie and stopped me in my tracks. I looked about for the source and found the haughty Persian, Colette. She was sprawled atop a low, flat monument, her limbs twisted into a yogic knot that made her look like a piece of abstract sculpture.

"I beg your pardon?"

"Magnificent, isn't he?" she repeated, twisting her head to an impossible angle so that she could lap up the last sight of your cathedral-like hindquarters: Chartres, but on four legs. We watched as you scaled first one mossy wall, then another, bound after effortless bound, hauling your treasures behind you like a trawler dragging a net. Then you were gone.

"Magnificent? Who do you mean?"

"Oh, come now," she laughed, huskily. "If I were a lexicographer, Oscar, I'd pair your name with 'diaphanous.' "

"I can't imagine what you're talking about."

"No?" she smirked, unfolding herself, slowly, slowly. It was like watching someone work out one of those Chinese puzzles, a tangle of interlocking rings. "You were eddying in his wake like a matchstick in a spring flood."

"Nonsense. I happened to be walking this way and—"

"Spare me, Oscar," she interjected, contorting herself into the letter Q. "I know your game, because he's my game, too. Our jolly ploughboy, I mean. I had him the other night, you know. He was insatiable. Insatiable."

I answered her with a sniff that was meant to convey indifference, but oh, my darling! Her words unseamed me from nave to chops.

"Insatiable, my dear, as though he was possessed. It was like playing a game of chance with three huge dice that wouldn't stop rolling, rolling, rolling. They spun so fast I'm amazed he didn't lift off."

Coarse!

"I still feel flush. What's more, I do believe he sowed his seed on fertile ground. I can feel that telltale stirring, Oscar. The yeast is proofing. There are worms in the can."

An unsavoury mix of metaphors, to be sure, but whiffs of verisimilitude rose from her wanton boast.

"Congratulations, my dear," I parried, lightly, for though my heart was breaking, I was damned if I would give her the satisfaction of seeing it. "How novel it must be for you to equate certainty with paternity."

She answered with a cruel laugh, then arranged herself in a figure 8. She held her skull between her hind legs, a grim homunculus, Hamlet and Yorick all in one.

"Let me confide something to you, Oscar, *fille à fille*. There are certain toms who are amenable to suggestion and who might, under the right circumstances or with adequate compensation, enter into some kind of arrangement with you. But Morrison isn't one of them. He doesn't know the meaning of the word 'detour.' He's about as flexible as a one-way ticket, and believe me, I know a thing or two about flexibility. You should come to my yoga classes, Oscar. I could teach you some tantric tricks that would help you channel that energy in a more productive direction."

Trollop!

"Thanks for your solicitude, Colette. Might I return the kindness by telling you that the judicious application of a conditioner would make you look less like a violated handbag. Good day, mademoiselle."

I showed her my tail.

"Longing is suffering, Oscar," she called after me, but I didn't accord her so much as a backward glance. I lifted my head. I checked the breeze for the scent of you. I took the advice of the wind. I was on my way. Full of longing and suffering gladly, I am now and will always be, your first and most loving admirer.

Your very devoted,
O.W.

LETTER: TO COLETTE FROM HER MOTHER

November 18

Chérie:
It is a truth, universally acknowledged, that nothing gives a mother greater joy than receiving a letter from her daughter, and that nothing breeds trepidation in the heart of a daughter like the arrival of a letter from her mother. As it has been my habit to perturb you by post at least once a day for these past several years, you must surely be curious about the silence that has latterly come over me. In case you are concerned or curious—and I have had no indication that you are—let me say straightaway that I have not been stricken with paralysis, nor with amnesia, nor with the sinus difficulties to which we Persians are sometimes prey. I have not been euthanized, nor have I been crated up and moved against my will to a less appealing *arrondissement*, as happened recently to one of my neighbours, a very strident Russian Blue, who now must bear the awful shame of living in the Marais. Can you imagine? *Quelle horreur!* No, *chérie*, rest assured that I am well and that I would have written, had not absolute and appalled amazement stayed my paw.

I have been accommodating myself, reluctantly, to the news that you are with kittens. On reflection, it is astonishing, given the life you lead and the company you keep, that this has not happened until now. I have also been adjusting to my own new status in the world. Slowly, and mostly by mouthing the word at myself in the mirror, I have admitted to the unsettling certainty that soon I shall be a grandmother. I would it were otherwise, but such things occur when one's daughter flees the nest at an early age, unformed, and before her education is complete. What I cannot arrive at, however, is an appropriate or perspicacious response to the stunning naïveté you betrayed in your last letter, the letter that precipitated my long silence.

You have always had a certain fondness for tough toms, for

rough trade, and evidently this damaging penchant remains intact. The tender way in which you write of his tattered ears, his icy eyes, his clenching jaw, his six broad toes and his well-oiled loins shows that you clearly believe you have staked some unique claim to his affections. Allow me to unsheath my claws and rake them over your pretty balloon of bliss. You are deluded if you think, for even a second, that it was your voice, your wit, your cream and white coat, or your nicely turned ankles that inspired his violations. Believe me, *chérie*, it was nothing more than your availability that made you so desirable, along with the unfettered billowing of In Heat, that alluring feline scent we queens sometimes make the mistake of wearing.

Worst of all, however, is your inexplicable optimism vis-à-vis the long term. I don't know whether to be alarmed or charmed that a daughter of mine, with your intelligence, with your experience, truly believes that any tom will ever be persuaded to be an equal partner in the nurturing of his spawn. A tom is a tom is a tom, and he has no more curiosity about his progeny than the wind has about the fluff it scatters when it passes through a field of wilted dandelions. A tom is like a delivery man whose only concern is to off-load his cargo as quickly as he can, who enjoys the feeling of a job well done and who then forgets all about it and moves onto the next assignment.

I will remind you, *chérie*, that I, too, am a daughter, and I know very well that the greatest satisfaction a queen can know is the pleasure of proving her mother wrong. But for once, be wise. Do not waste your time trying to second guess or subvert me, for I can assure you that, in this case, wrong is something I am absolutely not. God gave us toms so that kittens might be made, and God gave us queen mothers so that we might have help with their rearing. Nothing you can say will prevent me from coming to help you, for I am your mother, and, as you very well know, a mother's love is not easily dislodged or dissuaded.

Your loving,
Maman

ALICE B.

It was Voltaire, I do believe, who stressed that our first
responsibility is to our gardens. We must cultivate them, he
told us, and I, quixotically, have taken his advice to heart.
Here, in this place of rotting and dying, in this sunless season of bone-chilling winds, I saw to the generous scattering
of seeds. I did this full of the instinctive certainty and confidence that Gertrude would grow from one of them. And
now, with no evidence other than the thrilling descant of my
heart, I believe that somewhere, deep inside some swelling
womb, she has taken root. One day soon, as the proverb
promises, I will reap what I have sown. Between times, I must
manage what I have begun. Between times, I must nurture.
What a job that promises to be. Cooking and feeding, cooking and feeding: it is what I have always done, but now my
vocation is freighted with a new sense of urgency.

Satisfying hunger, in a place like Père-Lachaise, reminds
me of the very unpleasant years of the Second World War.
Then, Gertrude and I fled Paris and took up permanent
residence in the countryside. It was a time of great scarcity.
The Germans, in the piggy way of invading armies everywhere, had laid claim to the best of everything. Feeding oneself required considerable cunning, and the lessons of
adaptability I learned during those lean times have served
me well during my present tenancy. For it is as true here as
it was there that resourcefulness, luck and a few helpful con-
tacts go a long way to securing the wherewithal necessary for
a varied diet.

Regardless of one's situation, a joyful spontaneity in the
face of availability is the key to a happy career in cookery.
Give me but a rat and a lemon, and I will concoct a tasty
meal. However, I have been pleased to find that with fore-
sight, luck, the right goods for barter and the brazen assistance of Buttons, there are very few comestibles that cannot
be secured.

Buttons, Buttons. Tender Buttons! He is my sous-chef, my errand boy, my chief purser. I liked him from the moment I found him, famished and bony but full of resolve, a reject from his litter, a frisky young throwaway doing his best to simply scrape by. He had the look of one who knew the deepest meaning of hunger. I liked that. There's no one as loyal as someone whose hunger you've staunched, and loyalty I have always valued, even when it has been purchased.

If I am so keen an appreciator of fidelity, it is perhaps because the assistant who preceded Buttons was a traitorous piece of work. Héloïse! I can barely bring myself to mention her name. Yes, I do indeed mean the selfsame Héloïse who, once upon a two-legged time, round about a thousand years ago, achieved widespread notoriety as the tempting teenager who became the lover of her tutor, Abélard, and who bore him a son. Héloïse, who signed up for a stint in a nunnery to conceal the affair from her outraged guardian. Héloïse, who continued to entertain her big-brained beau in the convent until her protector, once he was in the know, arranged to have the roué castrated. Yes, that Héloïse, who, along with her paramour, is commemorated with a neo-Gothic monstrosity in the ultra-chic 7th division of Père-Lachaise.

Abélard is here as well, of course, and I can tell you that those two cut quite a swath after so many centuries of free-floating while waiting for translation. The sparks they set off when they met again! They glowed, they were the golden couple, the twosome everyone wanted to know, the Scott and Zelda of the moment. They were young, attractive, incandescent, and they enjoyed a long ascendant social season at the top of Fortune's wheel. Then came the day that history, that spicy radish in the crazy salad of time, repeated itself; the day that Abélard fell into the clutches of the menacing Ondine and was once again removed, howling and against his will, from the register of the procreative.

"What am I to do, what am I to do?" wailed the disconsolate Héloïse when she came hammering on my door on the very evening Abélard was taken. We were not closely acquainted—I knew her mostly because I was often engaged to provide the fare for the *fêtes* at which they were inevitably featured—but I was not surprised that she sought me out. My own history with Ondine, and the way I had willingly subscribed to her clipping service, was well known. Héloïse came to me because she needed to hear reassuring coos from a surviving veteran of the wars. These I did my best to provide, but I did not try to keep from her the truth of how her lover would return to her an altogether altered cat.

"You mean," she said, swallowing her sobs, "that he won't be a whole tom?"

"There, there," I answered, stroking her head. "It won't do to think of it like that. He'll still be exactly the same Abélard you've always loved. You might just have to find a different—how shall I put it?—a different focus for your relationship."

This remark, which I thought to be quite temperate and realistic, set her off on an extended jag of sputtering and wailing and carrying on.

"What shall I do?" she blubbered. "Whatever shall I do? No one will want to see us, no one will ask us out, no one will—"

"Come now," I interjected, "surely you don't think your friends are as fickle as that!"

"But I've seen it! I've seen what happens after Ondine! There's a taint you carry. Others shun you, it's as if you were cursed. You can't pretend you don't know what I mean, Miss Toklas. You of all—"

She stopped herself mid-sentence, hastily swallowed her unspoken words, hiccuped and gathered her composure.

"I shall have to work," she said, decisively. "I shall have to take a job. That's all there is to it. Miss Toklas, do you have any need of an assistant?"

This all happened shortly after Tristesse, who now and again had been able to lend me a faltering paw, took up her employment with Chopin, delivering the mail. I was feeling somewhat stretched, just then, and was also moved by the young queen's plight. She really did seem deflated and diminished.

"When could you start?"

"Tomorrow! Right now! Thank you, Miss Toklas," and she gave me a wet kiss. "You won't regret this!"

It was the first of her many lies.

But enough of Héloïse. She belongs to the past. I don't care to speak of her. It all worked out for the best, because now I have my Buttons, and he is loyal and he is lean, and that is a good thing, too, for his work obliges him to pass often, and with speed, through the narrow honeycomb of tunnels that twist and intersect beneath the cemetery: a complex maze of subterranean passageways and catacombs that connect one division to the next, dark corridors that permit those few creatures who are in the know—and who are not paralysed either by claustrophobia or by the frequent and unwavering regard of skulls—ready access to every quarter of our walled city, as well as to the crematorium. This is most vital because, in this place of few ovens, those grisly fires are pivotal to my vocational continuance.

Buttons is black. He wears creamy socks on his hind feet only and two white patches around his vacant, yellow eyes. Buttons is blind. He is also mute. The latter quality, of course, one always appreciates in an assistant. As to the former, it is, in his case, no disability whatsoever. Habituated from birth to an absence of light, Buttons quickly became conversant with the right-now, left-now imperatives of the catacombs. He never gets lost. He is intrepid and he is fast. If baking is required, for instance, he can make his way from my home in the 40th division to the crematorium in the 87th in under three minutes. Naturally, these forays are made only at night, when the body stokers have gone home and their cavernous furnace is cooling. So acute is Button's sense of touch that he can discern by a quick whisk of his tail when those glowing inner reaches are at an optimum temperature for the browning of whatever comestible is in his keeping. Likewise, he is gifted with a remarkable and infallible sense of smell that allows him to remove the goodies the very second they achieve the Platonic ideal of doneness.

Good food, simply prepared. That is what I have always advocated, and that is what I will continue to offer, even though there are those who say I am hopelessly out of step with the times. Oscar is forever telling me that I need to adapt to the whim of the moment, that I cling to my austere aesthetic to my peril.

"I was just at a function catered by Héloïse," he said to me recently, "and it was astonishing, a stunning amalgam of Thai influences and Korean references and discreet whispers from New Orleans, with a warm wind from Indonesia murmuring over the whole."

"Sounds frightful."

"Fusion in profusion, my dear. It's all the rage. You'd better catch up."

"Thank you, Oscar, for sounding the alarm, but I can still tell a flash in the pan from a full-scale fire. And remember, it was I who gave that simpering parvenu her start."

"That may be, my dear, but look at where she is today. And surely you should diversify! Simple catering is no longer sufficient to anyone's needs. Héloïse caters. She decorates. She consults. She's making a killing with her Lifestyle Management Packages."

Oh, Gertrude, my love, my puss, wherever you might be! Have I erred in engineering your re-entry into a world that accommodates such concepts as "Lifestyle Management Packages"? A world that accords status to someone simply because she can sculpt butter into swans and make a pile of pine cones resemble the Taj Mahal? Forgive me. I can only promise that, when you come, you will find me steadfast and unswerving. I float above fashion. And I still have my champions, my faithful clientele. Proust will not desert me, nor

Sarah Bernhardt. And there are some gustatory effects that the clever Héloïse will never be able to replicate, for I was canny enough to keep my secret ingredient under close guard. Héloïse would dearly love to know the special herb I fold into my batters and sauces, the additive that keeps them all coming back for more. But she won't find out any time soon.

And now to work. Miss Toklas, though *démodée*, still has much, much to do.

✤

PRESS RELEASE: ABÉLARD COMMUNICATIONS, INC.

For Immediate Release

Abélard Communications, Inc. is pleased to announce that, owing to unprecedented popular demand, Héloïse has scheduled a third presentation of her twice sold-out seminar "Bun in the Oven, Pussy in the Well: Designing Congenial Yet Stimulating Nurseries for Newborns." Registrants will learn creative and cost-effective ways to avail themselves of readily available materials to transform ordinary mausoleums into environments that are both cosily reassuring and intellectually stimulating.

Why settle for a plain old bassinet when your little ones can have a rigged and masted pirate ship?

Why not use a bit of bunting, a twist-tie and a fold or two of foil to craft a dangling mobile that will keep the kitties entranced for hours on end?

Are you are among the many in the gated community of Père-Lachaise who grapple with the decorating challenge of a leaded window that depicts a dour saint or glowering virgin? Héloïse will provide suggestions for turning any old down-in-the-mouth Apostle into a smiling elf or beneficent fairy godmother.

Why live in a bleak house when you can inhabit a house of mirth? Learn how your coming little one's life can be suffused from day one with the matchless aesthetic promulgated by Héloïse, the matchless aesthetic summarized in the maxim that has become her pledge and byword: "Nothing should look like what it really is."

The last two seminars sold out on the very day they were announced, so register early to avoid disappointment! This offer will not be repeated.

Biographical Information
About Héloïse

The story of Héloïse is among the most remarkable of our time. Born in the humblest of circumstances to poor immigrant parents, she early on showed a rare combination of flinty resolve and creative genius, the very qualities that have made her today's most sought-after Party Provider and Broker of Home and Office Environments. From her beginnings as a lowly caterer's assistant to her uncontested position at the top of the homemaking heap, Héloïse has striven for, and always attained, excellence.

Press kit available. Please address all inquiries to Abélard Communications, Inc.

-30-

LA FONTAINE'S VERSIFIED WALKING TOUR: SARAH BERNHARDT

If, one day, some psychologist sets out to chart and graph
The multitude of feline types extent upon the earth,
I hope she'll have some training in statistics and in math
To manage all the numbers, for of types there's not a dearth.

For instance, there's the gabby cat: loquacious, primed to chat,
Who uses several hundred words when most would stick to ten.
By contrast, still and taciturn, the meditative cat
Must live in strict accordance with the principles of Zen.

And then there's the conniving cat, an unrepentant cad,
Who's scheming and manipulating all the livelong day.
His opposite's the innocent, who's kittenish and glad
To conjugate her favourite verbs: "to sleep" and then "to play."

And certain cats espouse a friendly informality,
While other cats, more rigid, like to hold themselves aloof.
Let's not forget the show-off cat, whose "Hey, ma! Look at me!"
Will manifest in daring acrobatics on the roof.

The fat and clumsy cat, who fractures vases by Lalique,
Is balanced by the cat who, lithe and agile, blithely strides
On lofty rails so thin you'd never sneak a downward peek.
For him, no sweat! He'll pirouette, then homeward, angel,
    glide.

The psychic cat's antennae pick up otherworldly vibes,
The narcoleptic cat has just one setting, i.e. "Snooze,"
The whining cat is known as the kvetcher of the tribe,
And bell the cat who's bellicose: he's apt to blow a fuse.

The types I've listed here are just the fabled iceberg's tip.
I might go on forever, but economies of scale
Require the fist of rhetoric to loosen up its grip:
In other words, to engineer the ending of this tale.

My point—oh ye of little faith who thought we'd not arrive—
Is that there lives among us one whose gift is to engage
Her talents like a lariat, lassoing all these lives
Then strut her distillation for an hour on the stage.

I speak of Sarah Bernhardt, living legend, reigning star,
Acclaimed the greatest actress that the stage has ever seen.
Despite her missing leg, the plaudits ring out near and far:
All hail! She now approaches! Bernhardt! Tripod drama
queen!

⚜

ALICE B.

Were I—perish the thought—a realtor or some other like-
minded marketing type trying to persuade a client that Père-
Lachaise would be the perfect place to relocate the family or
incorporate a business, I would focus my pitch on the paucity
of news. No news, it seems to me, is the real selling point of
this place. It pleases me more than I can say that my days are
not cluttered by relentless reportage. Now and again, it is
true, an ill wind will deliver up a stray page of *Le Monde,* but one
glance is sufficient to know that dictators flex their muscles
just as they have always done, not caring that elsewhere, mere
miles away, another Ozymandias is being buried in the sand.

Tyrants come and tyrants go, and the only one who will
never be toppled is the tyrant Time. Time will rule forever,
blind and watchful, cruel and impartial. He will never relin-
quish his power, never relax his grip. However, if one is cunning enough, even so controlling an oligarch can sometimes
be persuaded to look away. There are opiates that will banish
Time, of course, and some have learned that prayer or med-
itation will suspend, if but fleetingly, his rule. Personally, I
have found the most direct route to the Time-Free Zone to
be dumb domestic routine. Not enough attention has been
paid to housework as an entry point to the State of Epiphany.
Sorting screws into cans; the slow methodical passing of a
feather duster over a knick-knack—laden shelf; the prising off
of baked-on grime from the scored and scoured surface of a

saucepan: any one of these activities, if accorded mindful attention, may lift one to that higher plane where one is, if only blinkingly, out of Time's sight.

I often find myself negotiating such a truncated treaty with Time as I prepare to cook. I begin, always, with a pantry inventory, and it sometimes happens, when I scan the shelves and cupboards of my larder, that I feel the loosing of those shackles. I release all the needless things of the world as I assess what is arranged before me, quickly tallying the sum of their parts, imagining how one element might be combined with another to alchemical effect and how it could all be changed again with the simple addition of some ingredient Buttons might find. This morning, however, I was pulled softly from one of my pantry trances by a warm and genial salute.

"Good morning, Miss Toklas."

Sarah Bernhardt!

"It's a fine day for November, Miss Toklas. No sign of rain."

So comely she was as she leaned in through my window, with her coat the colour of pewter and her three lovely legs, long and impossibly elegant.

"May I come in, Miss Toklas?"

Her voice! Perfectly pitched, a rare amalgam of smoke and crystal.

"I do hope you'll excuse the intrusion. Do you mind if I set this down?"

Her phrasing was so clear, so precise, that I had not even noticed how her maw was stuffed with a rat. A red trickle, sticky and discreet, oozed from the corner of its own thin lips. If memory serves, it was Demosthenes who filled his mouth with pebbles and shouted down the trumpeting surf, the better to hone his oratorical skills. That Demosthenes cut an impressive figure on the Aegean shore I have no doubt. But for all his elocutionary efforts and for all his pioneering enterprise in the field of speech pathology, he surely could not hold a candle to Sarah Bernhardt, the Queen of Articulation. And that is not the limit of her peerlessness.

There was never such a ratter as Sarah Bernhardt. She is, as anyone will tell you, our goddess of the hunt: Diana, but with whiskers. She is nimble and speedy, a living exemplum of the body's ability to accommodate its accidental losses, for she is wholly unhobbled by the ancient mishap that robbed her of a limb. The miraculous Sarah Bernhardt betrays not a trace of anything you might call a limp. Indeed, she trots along as jauntily on her three legs as do any of the rest of us on our full complement of four.

To happen upon Bernhardt in action and to study her killing ways with Rodentia is another way to arrest the rule of Time. Even Time, that most irascible of despots, stops in his tracks to marvel at how she makes the gruesome beautiful through her singular union of head and heart, theory and practice, theatre and commerce. It is true that flesh is torn and blood is spilled, but in such a way as to induce a state of almost mesmeric serenity. The depth and dimension of Bernhardt's Art would mitigate the murder even if the more pedestrian requirements of the gut were adjudged insufficient currency to purchase redemption. Her eyes become shade-shifters, flashing from amber to green to orange to black. Slowly, slowly, she beckons the victim to come hither, come hither, like some Arabian Nights temptress lifting veil after veil, crooning a rhythmic, sultry song. Curve and swerve, bend and sway, advance and retreat: and when at last she strikes, it is as though thought and action have become one, as though the quarry has forsaken selfhood and now belongs to Bernhardt and Bernhardt alone, its family and friends forgotten, its gods overthrown. Why, I have seen rats dance gleefully into her jaws of their own accord, like Cinderella stepping into the golden coach.

"Miss Toklas," said Sarah Bernhardt, when she had disabused herself of her oily cargo, "I have the Renaissance Revue planning committee coming for a noontime meeting, and I suppose that means I'll have to feed them lunch. Is there something you might do with this poor specimen? Nothing elaborate, of course, no need for any *en croûte* fripperies or any such thing."

"By all means," I answered, knowing exactly how I would proceed. "I'll fix something up quickly and have Buttons deliver it by 11:45. Will that suit?"

"You are too kind, Miss Toklas. A lifesaver, really."

Coming from anyone else, this would gave been gratingly ingratiating. However, Bernhardt is able to invest even the most transparent compliment with the kind of weight that makes one willingly suspend disbelief and simply take it as one's due.

"Oh, and Miss Toklas, there is another small matter of business, rather a delicate one. Have you a minute to talk, by the way?"   .

"Certainly."

"Good. You know, I think, how very partial I am to your cooking."

"You've always been very generous in your support."

"Only because the product warrants it, Miss Toklas. I have always insisted, as indeed I shall insist again this afternoon, that you be given the contract to provide catering services for our post-performance reception. How many years has it been now?"

"I've lost track. More than I'd care to number."

"Quite. It's a tradition that I value—I think we are far too fickle when it comes to keeping up our traditions, Miss Toklas—and I am prepared to fight to see that it endures. However, I feel obliged to tell you that there are a number of committee members who feel—and you must not take this as a slight, Miss Toklas—that it is time to try something new. You are probably aware that another catering service has recently launched itself on the scene, with a certain degree of success it must be said, and a few of the committee members have made it known—"

Sarah Bernhardt by night

And at this point, I interjected by clearing my throat and raising a paw. I was hardly surprised to learn that Héloïse was pressing her case, particularly since her cohort Abélard is a long-time and vocal planning committee member.

"I understand completely, Miss Bernhardt, and I appreciate your tact and honesty. I will say only that I am available and that if the committee chooses to engage my services, I will be very happy to provide the revue with whatever it requires."

"Thank you, Miss Toklas," she exhaled, clearly relieved to have that part of her mission out of the way. And then she was gone.

There was a time when I would have been deeply upset and hurt by such an exchange. I would have felt betrayed and sullied. But I know now that all that really matters is the steady nurturing and safe arrival of my Gertrude. Heaven knows I have plenty to keep me occupied in that regard. And as for Héloïse, well, she will get what she deserves, in the twists and turns of time. As shall I, and sooner rather than later; for soon, Gertrude will come.

⚜

ALICE B. COOKS: RATRAT TARTAR

Had there been more time and warning, and had I been able to take advantage of the oven, I might have settled on a roast or a fricassee or a casserole for Sarah Bernhardt's meeting. However, as prompt action was required, I chose instead the delightfully palindromic Ratrat Tartar, which is straightforward to prepare and a pleasure to present.

If there are many ways to cook a rat, there is also a multiplicity of methods for skinning one. Once you have secured the star player—and it is surely no accident that "star" spelled backwards spells what "star" spelled backwards spells—divest it of its pelt in your own preferred fashion. Eviscerate the miserable creature, then hang the meat until it is drained of all unwanted fluids.

While gravity is taking care of that grim necessity—allow perhaps fifteen minutes, depending on the size of the rat and your altitude—make the marinade. Take the juice of one lime, a minced shallot, a whisper of cilantro, a drop or two of soy sauce and a generous cutting of the finest hashish. Combine. Marinate the drained meat for half an hour.

At this point, you must make a decision about how best to proceed. If you have the time or the inclination, you could go the barbecue route. If you are feeling rather more like sashimi, slice the meat to an airy, carpaccio-like thinness and serve straight away. If you choose to do as I did and opt for a tartar, grind the meat, mound it into something that looks akin to a brain, decorate with a sprig or two of parsley and serve it up on a bed of kale arranged on a silver platter, with an accompaniment of Melba toast or buttered *tartines*.

This is a low-fat dish that is kind to your heart but is also toothsomely filling. A little goes a long, long way, and I have never known it not to please.

CONFIDENTIAL DOCUMENT

Minutes of the Meeting of the Planning Committee
Annual Renaissance Revue
November 20

Present

Mr. Abélard, Miss Callas, Miss Colette, Mr. Dukas and Miss Bernhardt. Miss Bernhardt served as Chair. Reynaldo, personal assistant to Miss Bernhardt, acted as recording secretary.

The meeting was called to order at 2:30 P.M.

Approval of Minutes of the Last Meeting

Miss Callas pointed out an error and asked that a correction be made to the discussion pertaining to catering services. She was quite sure she did not say, "Miss Toklas is a meddling cow," but rather, "Miss Toklas seems muddled, now." Correction noted. Mr. Abélard moved approval of the minutes, seconded by Miss Callas. Carried.

Discussion of Program for This Year's Revue

Mr. Dukas advanced a motion that the committee formally thank Miss Bernhardt for generously agreeing to undertake the direction of the revue. Seconded by Mr. Abélard. Carried.

Miss Bernhardt presented a draft outline of this year's revue, to be presented at the Columbarium Theatre on Christmas Eve. It is a "back to basics" program intended, she said, "to allow the revue to regain some of the credibility it may have lost after last year's unfortunate episode." The show will consist of songs, sketches and *tableaux vivants*. Miss Bernhardt asked for the committee's input.

Mr. Dukas said that he would be happy to make the score and the scenario available once again for "The Sorcerer's Apprentice." He noted that he had heard from many audience members who were surprised and disappointed that it had been stricken from last year's revue, especially since it was a perennial favourite. All present voiced strong support for this idea.

Miss Colette pointed out that as a bumper kindle of kittens will be arriving in the week after the revue and that many of the participants will be yeastily swollen, one of the *tableaux vivants* should reflect that reality. She volunteered to concoct an appropriate scenario.

Mr. Dukas said he thought this a wonderful idea and volunteered to advance it as a formal motion.

Miss Bernhardt said that no motion would be necessary. While she was happy to hear any and all suggestions, she asked that it be formally noted in the minutes that final approval would rest wholly with her. "Democracy," she said, "is the archenemy of Art."

Mr. Abélard also favoured the idea of a *tableaux vivant* anchored in the here and now but felt impending motherhood did not have the dramatic heft necessary to engage a wide public. He suggested that a demonstration from Miss Héloïse on the artful carving of radish roses might have broader appeal.

Miss Colette said that her knife was dull and wondered if Mr. Abélard would care to "bend over and be my whetstone."

Mr. Abélard requested that the committee resolve the question of who would provide food services at the post-performance reception and again suggested that Héloïse might be an appropriate choice, given that she is now so very much of the moment and that she is becoming "the caterer of choice."

Miss Bernhardt interjected, firmly, to move that the catering contract be put out to tender. Seconded by Mr. Dukas. Mr. Abélard and Miss Callas voted against the motion. Mr. Dukas, Miss Colette and Miss Bernhardt voted in its favour. Carried.

Mr. Abélard excused himself and left to attend a business meeting.

Other Business

Miss Bernhardt asked that the following statement be read into the minutes: "There have been suggestions that the revue has become too establishment driven and elitist. This year, to address the concerns of the Reform Lobby, we will open the revue to cats who are untranslated.

Mr. Dukas and Colette voiced their support for this initiative.

Miss Callas said, "It's your funeral," and repeated her remark at the request of the recording secretary before moving adjournment. Seconded by Mr. Dukas, who also thanked Miss Bernhardt, on behalf of the committee, for the generous luncheon and wondered if there might be another slice of fudge. Sadly, there was not.

Meeting adjourned at 3:55 P.M.

La Fontaine's Versified Walking Tour:
Mademoiselle Lenormand, Fortune Teller

A fatal curiosity attaches to cat kind:
We're victims of the constant question, Why?
But all the interrogatives that clutter up cats' minds
Grow pale beside the human need to pry.
Yes, all the niggling wonderings that make us blindly jump—
For looking leaches leaping of its mirth—
Are more than amply magnified within the clods who stump
As bipeds on the byways of the earth.

It wasn't, after all, a cat, who at the snake's behest
Devoured the fruit that spread the primal stain.

And neither did some feline felon smash Pandora's chest,
Thus loosing on the world what it contained.
Cats are disinclined to guess the ending of the tale:
They let the future take the path it likes.
Humans always long to look behind the temporal veil,
To see what's coming at them down the pike.

Now, here lies one whom Joséphine—Napoleon's *amour*—
Engaged to tell her what the cards foretold.
She shuffled them, she laid them out and then began to purr:
"No hunger written here. No need. No cold."
It was so. That trio never spoke the empress's name,
Till on the day she drew her final breath:
Then hunger, need and cold rushed in to stake, at last, their
  claim.
That's death, my dears. That's death. That's death. That's death.

CHOPIN: NOCTURNE FOR THE FEAST DAY OF ST. CECILIA

Blessed Cecilia, patron of music and guardian of all its many
makers, I, Chopin the cat, thank you for the blessing of this
still, cold night. I thank you, too, for the gift of this taut and
cloudless sky, and for all it contains and all it spills down—the
do-mi-sol of the chanting seraphim:

  Hail, oh bright Cecilia,
  Hail oh virgin proud,
  Let no night conceal you,
  Let each voice sing loud.
  May each chord and unison
  Ring out round and rich,
  Bless us with your benison,
  Keep us well on pitch.

May I also take the opportunity to thank you, St. Cecilia, for whatever assistance and intervention you have been able to provide vis-à-vis the project on which I have been so long embarked and which I have mentioned to you on several previous, prayerful occasions. I refer to my ambition to assemble a complete set of playing cards, so that I might satisfy a craving of long standing and cut a swath at the whist table. Day after day I make my way to the weathered stone that marks the resting place of Mademoiselle Lenormand, the celebrated fortune teller and psychic advisor to the Empress Joséphine. Her many admirers and adherents often leave stray clubs and diamonds, aces and hearts, on her grave when they come to pay their respects

Slowly, patiently, I have gathered up these cards, one by one, suit by suit, gradually building up my inventory towards the requisite fifty-two. Just yesterday I added the ace of spades to my cache. Now, I am but one heart short of a full deck. No doubt, oh all-seeing St. Cecilia, you appreciate the aptness of this, given the way my heart-of-old was wrested from my chest and ferried off to Warsaw, just prior to my more substantial interment here in Père-Lachaise. Nor was this irony lost on Miss Toklas, with whom I crossed paths this afternoon when I was out on my rounds. She chuckled when she heard my news.

"Which heart is yet to come?"

"The queen."

"Ah," she chortled, "the missing queen of hearts! Something we have in common, Chopin."

We fell into step and ambled in a southerly direction down the avenue Patchod, heading towards the tangle of streets in the 40th division, which is where she makes her home. It is a hilly neighbourhood that presents particular challenges for postal delivery, as this section of Père-Lachaise has been capriciously contoured to accommodate geography rather than to appease the fettering sensibilities of planners. The various lanes and passageways are woven among gullies and rises. They peter out with no apparent reason, then start again a hundred metres on. They are labyrinthine, helter-skelter; random, like dangling spaghetti strands hurled at the kitchen wall by some antic al dente inquirer.

"Tell me, Chopin," she asked, as we trotted along, "what do you miss most about *then*?"

"I beg your pardon?"

"What do you miss about *then*? Miss most of all."

"Then?"

"Don't prevaricate, Chopin. You remember your upright life just as well as I remember mine."

"Enough to say that I was rarely described as 'upright.' "

"But what do you miss? What lack rankles most?"

This did not strike me as a productive line of inquiry, but I knew there was no point in ignoring her question or sloughing it off. Miss Toklas—witness her patient waiting for Miss Stein—is the embodiment of tenacity.

"Is it music?"

"It would surely be music if music were absent, but my head is full of the stuff, day and night, waking and dreaming. The difference between now and then is that I'm no longer equipped to realize its execution."

"No piano or orchestra, you mean."

"To say nothing of opposable thumbs, Miss Toklas. It doesn't matter. In fact, I prefer it. The transference from pure thought to notation, and then from notation to per-formance, is inevitably misshapen and stumbling, like the Golem thudding down the streets of Prague. What's the best that one can expect? That listeners will experience a moment of transcendence, I suppose. That's an off chance at best, since for most concert-goers, the music is an inconvenience to be endured until the intermission, when gossip and cham-pagne are accorded their proper precedence. And as for the composer and performer, well, they are hardly nobler. What is the final object of their striving if not the adulatory approval of the throng?"

"You're too prickly by half, Chopin. We all crave approval."

"But there is no more meretricious medium for its conveyance than applause! I recall long, deep bows, then reassuming the vertical and looking out over the crowded hall, only to realize that I had cast my pearls before seals. There they sat, row after row, barking and beating their flippers, begging for another fish to be thrown. You wonder what I miss, Miss Toklas? Not that. Certainly not that."

The rules of conversation, to say nothing of courtesy, required that I return the question to her court, but there was little point in prolonging the volley. We all know what—or rather, who—she misses most of all. About this, Miss Toklas has never been anything other than frank and candid. And so we settled into a companionable silence until we came to the crossroads where our paths would diverge.

"Goodbye, Chopin."

"Safe home, Miss Toklas."

"Would you come for dinner? Some time next week?"

"I would be delighted."

"I'll send word with Tristesse."

We went our ways. Alone, I marshalled my thoughts for inspection. Why, I wondered, had I been so withholding about my own truth? You know it well enough, St. Cecilia. You can break open my heart as easily as if it were a fortune cookie and read what's written there. Of course, you know that it is indeed music that I long for, music more than anything else: music that is real and dimensional and public; garish and moving and loud. But to name that ache, to give it voice, would be to hold a drill to the wall of the dam I have worked long and hard to build, and that I will not do.

What do you miss most about then, Chopin? In the final analysis, the question is gratuitous, for then was then, and all that matters about then is that then is not now. Now is now, and now I have my letters and the music in my brain that will not stop and that rises in crenellated waves like heat from the pavement, rises up and passes through the seams of my skull to become one with the air: music that will never, ever, be heard by anyone other than me.

"Good evening, Chopin," called the frisky Isadora, dervishing around me as I turned up my walkway.

"Good evening, Miss Duncan. Should you be exerting yourself so strenuously? In your condition, I mean."

"Don't be such a stick-in-the-mud," she laughed, as she spun and whirled, then launched an impressive jeté. "I've never felt better! Never once in my life have I felt better than I do now!"

I watched the pale florescence of her ribbons trail behind her as she capered off into the dark, watched the fluttering of those long, bright strands until there was nothing left to see but the night and nothing to hear but my own music. I unleashed a waltz. I gave it a name: "The sound of one cat dancing."

Part II

December: Lost and Found

La Fontaine's Versified Walking Tour: Thus Far

Though physics is a frequent source of reeling stupefaction,
Most of us can grasp, I think, that action breeds reaction.
This lesson's in the Bible, too, I recollect it goes:
A cat will live to reap one day exactly what she sows.
Miss Toklas, in November, tilled and planted every field,
And now it's come December, she anticipates the yield.
But which of every scattered seed will root in fertile ground?
And which will sprout the miracle of lost transformed to
  found?
And which will bloom to bear the fruit to lure her love, long
  gone?
And will Miss Stein come home at last? Read on, good cats.
  Read on.

⚜

Alice B.

And once again, and just last night, Gertrude floated
through my dreams: a dream in which all my lives and times
were compressed into one. Dressed in the catsuit that has
been my dependable costume lo these many, empty years, I
lay sprawled on the stone on which our two names have been
carved and watched a little girl coming along the path. At
first, I thought she was a child like any other, but as she drew
near, I could see that she was, in fact, me; that is to say, she
was the me I used to be, when I lived in another country, in
another century.

I watched my two-legged, younger other as she broke into
a skipping gait. She bounced along for a few metres, then
stopped mid-stride, arranged her features into a mask of
gravity, thrust her hands into her pockets and proceeded in
my direction with a measured, stately tread. From her

demeanour and from her outfit—wide-brimmed black hat, long black wool coat, ankle-length black skirt, black worsted stockings, black shoes of patent leather—it was clear that she (and already I thought of her in the third person rather than the first) was a child on whom the habits of mourning had been imposed. Somewhere, I surmised, there would be the usual grown-ups, placing the usual flowers, observing the usual obsequies, as a body was deeded to the earth. Little Alice, bored with their demonstrations of grief and not yet schooled in the social niceties that attach to dying, had slipped away to wander on her own, just as any child might.

I broadcast a message into the air—*over here, girl, over here*—and my thought waves must have brushed her antennae, for she turned, looked, smiled. She took a step towards me, hand poised to caress, then stopped abruptly and pulled back, as if remembering some old admonition about the dangers of petting strange animals. She redirected her hand to her pocket, reached in and extracted a small container.

"Alice!"

A voice, agitated and harried, in the distance. She ignored it, opened her little bottle and drew from it a bubble-blowing wand, dripping with soapy liquid.

"Alice!"

The voice again, now more insistent. I watched, fascinated, as the she-who-was-me held the wand to her lips and blew. The goopy liquid resisted her breath, then bulged into a fluttering oblong before achieving release—the easiest of births—and becoming a greasy, bobbing sphere, streaked through with rainbows. The new bubble tested the air, hitched itself to the first passing breeze and rose up and up and up.

"Alice!"

A note of urgency now. The child heaved a sigh, screwed the cap back on her bottle of suds, replaced it in her pocket and turned to go.

"*À bientôt,*" she said to me, as she ran in the direction of the voice.

"*À bientôt,*" I answered, but sadly, for I knew better than she that it would not be long, in the grand scheme of things, before we would meet again, and not in any way she could ever expect. Young Alice ran off on her two pretty legs and passed out of view around a corner.

I turned my attention to the bubble, which was enjoying what I knew would be a brief career as an aerialist. It skidded over the smooth surface of the blue, refracting the light, first from one angle, then another, and I saw, much to my delight, that it contained *her* face—that Gertrude was peering down at me from the lighter-than-air bathysphere, with her strong centurion features, her deep, bright eyes. I stood on my hind legs, holding up my two front paws in a gesture of welcome. I spoke her name, and an obliging breeze brought her into my embrace. But, of course, my touch was too much for the bubble to bear, and it burst into a splatter of soap, whispering a single word, just one syllable, spoken in her own commanding, unmistakable voice: "*Soon.*" A beautiful word. Full of both ambiguity and assurance, and so sensual to pronounce, the way it forces the lips into a kiss. Which is what I did. I sent her a kiss on the back of the word "soon."

When the bubble broke and I awoke—with "*soon, soon*" in my ears—I lay quietly, listening to the sounds of the not-yet-dawn (Tristesse snoring, the percussive rain, the low thunder of the day's first Métro, rumbling far beneath this bank of bones) and taking stock of my body. The corporal inventory uncovered two distinct aches: one in my heart and one between my legs. The tightness in the chest, that mock angina, I know very well: it is a physiological register of my longing. The other visitation, the nether throb, is a more recent occurrence, its source more oblique. Ever since I engineered the dawning of our present golden age of fertility, I have been hosting such pangs, a harmonic response to the twinges and agues every queen in kindle now endures, with varying degrees of gladness. A phantom pregnancy. It amazes me that I, of all cats, am susceptible to such a haunting; I, who happily arranged to have my purse stitched up so that no tom would try to tender there his coins. Even so, it seems there is still a thick bass string, deep within me, that vibrates sympathetically when I see all my sisters swelling.

Never do I feel this bond of ponderous unanimity more acutely than at the morning yoga sessions Colette has been leading for queens-in-waiting. It was never my intention to be an active participant in these contortionist classes. My intention was to watch from the margins, waiting to distribute my embryo-enhancing snacks when all the stretching and the twisting was over and done. But Colette would not brook my holding back.

"We'll have no onlookers here, Miss Toklas. Come along and join in! This will do you good."

Colette is not to be trifled with. For three weeks now I have done her bidding, and I am bound to say I feel no different in my body than when I began. Nonetheless, I persist.

"This limbers the lumbar," our yogi will say, hiking her hind end skyward and using her upper body to describe an 80-degree angle, so that she resembles a hirsute ski slope, "and that is good, for unless the lumbar is limber, one lumbers."

Gertrude, when she arrives, will be surprised, and perhaps rather pleased, to find herself heir to a whole new set of physical possibilities. Feats of running, jumping and balancing that have never been in the repertoire of an upright walker are standard cat issue. I shall never forget how thrilled I was the first time I scaled a tree, gripping its bark as easily as I might once have done the railing of an escalator. And the amazing suppleness; at least, amazing when compared to the accustomed rigidity of the two-legged life. Of course, there are some who are more supple than others. Compared to many of my sisters, even in their advanced stages of pregnancy, I am the soul of calcification.

"Remember, my dears," Colette will admonish, "this is not a competition. Proceed at your own pace, taking the stretch only as far as you can comfortably go!"

Try though I might to take this to heart, I cannot help but send sidelong glances at the other students. Nor can I help but notice that they are always much more flexible than I.

"Don't strain, Miss Toklas!" Colette will command, as I heave and grunt to hoist my left rear leg as high as Isadora, or to flatten my chest to the earth with the same fluent fluidity as Sarah Bernhardt.

Sometimes, a meditative calm takes me over, and I allow my mind to wander. Often it comes home, wagging its tail behind and with Gertrude in tow. While executing the pose called "downward-facing dog," I will be visited by the memory of how much she loved our chihuahua Pépé and our two poodles, both named Basket, and will wonder, with some trepidation, how she will warm to this place, which must be the only public space in Paris where dogs are specifically prohibited.

Or else, while watching how easily Maria Callas can braid herself into something like a challah, I will be struck by how "yoga," writ in reverse, is "a goy," and my mind will surge with the image of Gertrude, the wandering Jew, striding through an endless desert, exiled from the promised land, which is the land of my love. And when Colette, praising Callas's elasticity, laughs and says, "Go, diva," the words elide for me to "Godiva."

Gertrude, Gertrude, wherever you might be, do you remember Godiva? She was our car, our Ford, our open-air Ford. For you, it was always a Ford, a Ford or nothing, do you remember? Do you remember Godiva with her top down, and we two motoring along, through the maddeningly narrow cobbled streets of Paris or down rutted country roads shaded by the sweep of plane trees? Through whatever the elements in our thick greatcoats and our knitted watch caps, or in our batik sundresses and our wide-brimmed bonnets, motoring along with you at the wheel, always you at the wheel, looking all around, gesturing extravagantly, talking, talking; and me, always me, silent at your side, my eyes fixed squarely on the road, hands gripping the dash but always ready to squeeze the bulb of the klaxon horn to warn away chickens, dogs, peasants.

You drove, always, for you were made of the stuff of steering, and I was born to be a passenger. *Your* passenger, my absent beloved, my wandering Jew. Your passenger, only. With you at the wheel and me at your side, we drove and drove. The adventures we had! The adventures we will have, and soon, my love. Soon and soon and soon.

LETTER: SARAH BERNHARDT TO MARCEL PROUST

December 3
Palazzo Phèdre

My dear Monsieur Proust:
It has been some time since last we met, and I hope you will tolerate the present intrusion. The last occasion on which we spoke was fully a year ago, at the interval of the Renaissance Revue. You were making for the exit. No one could blame you for leaving early. The Molière experiment was a disaster, miserably misguided. An atrocity. A crime against Art. Against decency. I shudder to recall it.

"Molière sells," the damn fools clamoured, "Molière always sells!" What none of them seemed willing or able to acknowledge is that the four-legged Molière who walks among us now, leering and drooling and swatting at gilded butterflies, is a highly diluted version of the original. Our Molière, sad to say, has suffered badly in translation. We have been saddled with a Molière who is, as anyone can see, more than a few footlights short of full illumination. The title alone should have been sufficient warning: *Les Purrgeois Gentilhommes.* Really!

Was it that execrable evening that inspired your decision to retreat to your room and never stir again from the safety of its confines? It may well have been, as I'm quite sure you've not been seen in public since that night. For whatever they are worth, I hope you will accept my reassurances that this year will be very, very different. I feel confident that you will be well pleased with the results, if you can bring yourself to attend.

But forgive me, dear Monsieur Proust. *Excusez-moi.* This blithering carrying-on has nothing to do with my purpose in writing to you now. I have a matter of the utmost urgency about which I should like to solicit your advice. There has been a break-in here at the Palazzo Phèdre, and I have suffered a most grievous loss. I would rather not consign the details to a letter but would prefer it if we could meet face to face, the better to pass on the details of the crime. Then, should you feel able to assist me with an investigation, we can outline the terms and conditions of your engagement. Do I have your permission to ferry some lunch to your home tomorrow, so that we may discuss this further?

I shall arrange for Miss Toklas to cater. I know she is no longer as much in fashion as once she was, but there is no one like her when it comes to preparing a simple and filling dish in the provincial style, which is what I have in mind. Simple is best, don't you think? And I am very much in the mood these days for nourishing, full-bodied meals. Such a hunger has come over me latterly! It is to be expected for, as you may have heard, I am with kittens. Happily, it has been the easiest of pregnancies. Indeed, I feel as though the energies of my youth have been returned to me threefold!

Do say yes, Monsieur Proust. Say yes by return post. I look forward very much to seeing you tomorrow at noon.

Yours very sincerely,
S.B.

✣

Proust Questionnaire: Two

Q: Who has stolen Sarah Bernhardt's leg?

A: Sometimes, when the light penetrates the narrow slats of my shutters—the moody half-light so particular to this time of year, that light which is as feeble and wan as a failing consumptive—and when it arranges itself, fastidiously, in narrow, angled pennants upon the screens and chairs and couches, like so many scarves laid out by an indecisive debutante dressing for the ball; then, that anaemic light, as it makes its slow pilgrimage from one end of the room to the other, will seem to warm and awaken in these, my inanimate companions, their secret but indomitable will to breathe, to move. Perhaps I will see a chaise take a baby step forward, or a table hop on its clawed feet, or a lamp give a stiff and courtly bow. Then I will be moved once again to consider how guilty we are of the most straitened and soured provinciality when we dismiss the possibility of soulfulness in all the things of this earth, whether or not they are made of flesh; for do we not diminish ourselves when we deny anything, however insignificant it might seem, the possibility of potentiality?

It is at such animistic moments as these that I detect a welling in the core of my being of something that feels like pity: pity for my door. In the gloom of my room I parse my arse and wonder if, in its secret heart—wherever a door's heart might beat, next to its hinges, beside the latch, under its knob—it mourns the limitations I have imposed upon it. Like any of its colleagues, in any place and at any time, my door has two stances: the open and the closed. If a door is denied the reasonable opportunity to be, throughout its working day, first one thing and then the other, is it not a door that is leading only half a life? Do I do my door a disservice by commanding it to remain, for very long stretches of time, in the shut position? For any unexpected hammering on the face of the door that looks out at the world is met, from this inner side of the divide, with only silence

Knock, knock.
  Who's there?
Cat gut.
  Cat gut who?
Cat gut your tongue?

Tinkers, higglers, evangelists, petition passers: anyone of these, after they have rapped with the knocker and received no reply, might put an ear to the door—poor door, aching to show off its only trick—and give themselves over to the aural equivalent of squinting. But no matter how long or hard they listen, no matter what anguished facial contortions they assume as they screw up their ears, no sound will come back to them, no sound other than the echo of their tapping: no lifting of the latch, no rattle of the key, no turning of the handle.

The only knocks that stir in me an answering impulse are the timid rappings of the mail girl, and the rhythmic whack— long, long, short, short, long—that signals the arrival of Buttons, the blind and mute tom who comes twice a week bearing victuals from the good widow Toklas. Buttons is one I am always glad to see, and not just because his name contains the phonetic haunch of my lingering preoccupation, the anatomical focus of my days. No, I welcome him into the Holy See—which should, I suppose, given my habitual optic, be written as "holey see"—because while my chosen work of tunnelling my way into the secrets of the heart may appear to be a wholly static enterprise, it is not without its stresses and strains, and I do work up a considerable appetite. When Buttons knocks, therefore, I grant my door the relief of a brief opening, and it enjoys a similar respite to admit those occasional clients who are needful of my services as a private investigator. Today, I opened a new case that I shall file in the B drawer of my cabinet. To wit: that of Miss Sarah Bernhardt.

⚜

Transcript:
Sarah Bernhardt's Interview with Marcel Proust, P.I.

December 4

S.B.: Thank you, Monsieur Proust, for agreeing to see me, and on such short notice, too. I really am most distraught. My! What a charming home you have, and how wise of you to ration your sunlight in this way. It can be so wearing on chintz. Don't even bother offering me a chair, I'd rather stand. I think so much better on my feet. However, if you don't mind, perhaps my secretary, Reynaldo, could take a seat, the better to take dictation. He will provide you with a very complete account of our meeting.

As you might have guessed, Monsieur Proust, it is one of life's unavoidable and unpleasant surprises that brings me here today, and it is my hope that I can borrow from you, if you are willing, perhaps half a cup of your sagacity. Or, if you would rather, we could effect a trade. I will give you the benefit of my acquired intelligence, if you will give me some of yours. Does that sound like a fair bargain? Good. Here then, is my advice to you, Monsieur Proust: never fall in love with a balloonist. Had I not done so, I would not be troubling you today.

The balloonist in question was none other than Rossini. Ah, Monsieur Proust, you do your professional best to remain impassive, but I saw just now a look of surprise pass over your countenance. You are too young to have known him as he was, once upon a time. Handsome, swarthy, Italianate, passionate. He was one of my great loves, much older than I, of course, but so charming! So dashing and gallant! He fell in love with me from the other side of the footlights, as so many have. He sent flowers. He sent fish heads. It was spring. The air was heady with the smells of rot and recrudescence and the oozing of atavistic juices. Before I could say *"Lei mi piace molto,"* I was head over heels in love.

On a day when the chestnut trees were herniating under the weight of their blossoms, Rossini came to me, blindfold in paw, and said, *"Bellissima,* today I have arranged for you a little surprise!"

I managed a smile, even though I loathe nothing so much as a surprise. In life, as in Art, preparedness is everything.

"Caro," I giggled, calling on my every acting skill to project delight and suppress alarm, "couldn't you give me the tiniest of clues?"

"A little al fresco dining experience, *bella,"* he answered, with a sly grin.

Somewhere, Monsieur Proust, I have a catalogue of my aversions: "surprises" is at the head of the list, followed closely by "picnics." Why did God give us roofs, if not to spare us the necessity of eating outside? However, as the rebel passion had overthrown the government of good sense, I blithely donned the blindfold and allowed myself to be led along.

"Ecco!" he said, when we had reached our secret destination, and he helped me step into what felt like a wicker laundry hamper; which, as it turns out, is exactly what it was. Monsieur Proust, you are a tom, but you may still be able to apprehend that a queen who feels as intensely as I, when she

decides to promenade along *les chemins d'amour*, comes to believe that the laws of physics no longer bind her. In the early days of my association with Rossini, I was deluded enough to think that gravity had commuted my life-term sentence to the prison called terra firma; that he had signed my pardon and allowed me to float, freely and at will. So, I thought nothing of it when I felt myself leaving the ground behind and rising up, rising up. Imagine my surprise, once the blindfold was removed, to find that my sense of ascension was not an emotive figment but was literally so, and that I was looking down upon the earth, some fifty feet below.

"*Sopresa!*" he crowed.

On my list of aversions, Monsieur Proust, after surprises and picnics, you will find heights. *Mon dieu!* Imagine, then, my horror when all three of my phobias were hitched up together and were dragging me helpless after them.

"But you are nervous, *carissima!*"

"Nonsense, darling! I tremble with delight!"

"Fear nothing! I am expert at this, and, in any case, you can see that we are fastened to the earth by this security rope."

And this was so. The cable that anchored us was handily knotted to the thick trunk of an oak. It showed no sign of strain when the balloon pulled and tugged against it.

"And, *bella gatta*, look at the feast I have prepared for you!"

It was, truth be told, a magnificent spread. Pâtés and cheeses, apricots and pears, breast of pigeon, brandy and petit fours, champagne. I was deeply impressed by his resourcefulness, which, I hasten to add, was not limited to the food; for the conveyance in which we rode was equally ingenious. Have you any idea how many helium-filled condoms are required to hoist so freighted a basket into the air? Hundreds and hundreds! Looking up at them all floating above us, I felt as a fish must when he swims beneath an enormous, undulating sea anemone.

Love and champagne are powerful opponents to any kind of resistance, Monsieur Proust, and it wasn't long before they had worn me down. I constructed my future as Signora Rossini; planned how I would gladly give up my life in the theatre and give over my days to the gathering up and laundering of condoms, in order that we might take many more pretty rides together. In a moment of mad inspiration I chose to reward my swain by administering a favour which few queens, anywhere, can claim to have disbursed at so lofty a height.

Dear Monsieur Proust, are you following all this? I have given you no time at all to ask questions, but I feel I am being very thorough. I believe it is part of police procedure to inquire whether the plaintiff has any enemies. Among our own kind, I am happy to say, I assuredly do not. However, it is equally certain that the families of the many rats I have dispatched over the years are not so kindly disposed to me. It was surely they, therefore, who waited until I was enmeshed in the business of pleasuring my balloonist before gnawing through the security rope, which, you will recollect, was all that kept us from leaping into the full embrace of open space. I felt a sudden jerk and thought I heard a high-pitched cheer, then realized, at that very moment, that we were floating free.

"Merda!" cursed the usually self-composed Rossini, leaving me in mid-kiss to peer over the edge of the basket. I joined him and was appalled by the sight of the retreating earth. The wind drove us persuasively in a southerly direction, and it would not be long before we found ourselves outside the walls of Père-Lachaise. I prepared myself to test the old equation about cats, heights and happy landings.

"No, no!" said my pilot. "I shall save us," and he began a series of complicated manoeuvres, adjusting various ropes, tugging various pulleys; but whatever plan he had in mind was scuttled by a loud report from the undulating forest of latex overhead. It was a sharp POP, like a windfall chestnut hitting the pavement. Then came another, and another, and another.

POP! POP! POP!

"Ma cosa?" demanded Rossini, as his makeshift balloons began to explode. I forced myself to look down and saw,

much to my horror, that the upper reaches of the trees below us were filled with rats, rats armed with peashooters.

POP! POP! POP!

"Do something!" I shrieked. But Rossini, clutching his eye, had collapsed to the floor of the basket and lay among the cheese rinds and rusk crumbs. Blood and something viscous oozed from his seeing socket. At that point, instinct joined hands with common sense and took over. I was never a student of physics but I knew, instinctively, that I would have to make the basket lighter to make it more buoyant. I began to jettison what was left of our picnic: glasses, plates, hamper, bottles. We rose commensurately, but not high enough to escape the upward hail of projectiles.

Another POP! Another! We were almost clear, but something else would have to go. I looked at Rossini, lying there inert, and two things were plain to me. One was that he was a cat of considerable girth and that he had been working hard to hold in his gut during our courtship. The other was that I could not simply obey my first impulse and heave him over. Selfless and self-reliant as always, I looked to myself for the solution.

You may have heard, Monsieur Proust, that when we are *in extremis* we are capable of extraordinary acts of courage. I am the limping proof that this is so, for there and then, with the half-blinded Rossini before me and the sound of popping condoms all around, I sized up my left rear leg. It looked to be the requisite weight. Summoning all the visualizing powers that are the gift of a life on the stage, I seized my limb in my jaws and pretended it was a rat.

NOTE FROM M.P.

There follow many, many more descriptive pages. The enormous pain, the perilous descent, the lucky recovery of the limb by Miss Toklas; its return, elaborate preservation and eventual installation above her fireplace: all these events are recounted in great detail, as is Miss Bernhardt's shock at finding that someone has latterly broken into her mansion and heisted the grisly souvenir.

Who has taken Sarah Bernhardt's leg?

S.B.: To anticipate your question, Monsieur Proust, I have not admitted anyone who is unknown to me to Palazzo Phèdre. I do not associate with known criminal elements. I beg your pardon, Reynaldo? Morrison? What has Morrison to do with this? Yes, it's true, he did happen by a few weeks back.

Excuse me, Reynaldo, I don't see that what passed between me and Mr. Morrison has any bearing on the case. He was interested in one thing only, and it wasn't my leg.

It is a world full of unsavoury types and individuals, as I'm sure you know, Monsieur Proust, and there is a black market for just this kind of gruesome memento. I could not bear it if my limb were to become part of some circus sideshow. I want not only to safeguard myself from such embarrassment and calumny but to ensure that my kittens will have what is rightfully theirs. It is no accident that the first syllable of "legacy" is what it is. Monsieur Proust, I want you to recover my leg, and soon.

NOTE FROM M.P.

For hours after Madame Bernhardt's departure, her clarion voice echoed round my room. Now, curled into my accustomed posture, I inhale the steadying redolence that is me, myself and I. I focus on the quiet mantra of my heart—go deep, go deep, go deep—*and project these questions onto the screen of my attention:*

> *Who has stolen Sarah Bernhardt's leg?*
> *Who has stolen Bonne Maman's book of spells?*
> *Are these random acts, or somehow connected?*

The heart knows, and it tells me where the answer lies. Go deep, go *deep, and that is just what I shall do, with my nose to what is not exactly a grindstone but is nonetheless the source of all my grist.* Go deep. *I go.* Go deep. *I go.* Deep. Deep. Deep.

❖

SARAH BERNHARDT

AND COMPANY

proudly present the
99th Annual
RENAISSANCE REVUE

with
Music ❧ Dance ❧ Drama
Refreshments ❧ Door prizes

Midnight sharp on Christmas Eve at the
Columbarium Theatre

LETTER: OSCAR WILDE TO JIM MORRISON

December 8

My Darling Jamz:
It has not escaped my attention that you have, to date, demonstrated an unmistakable apathy to my wheedlings, vis-à-vis a date. You have not said yes. You have not said no. You have not said maybe. You have not so much as sneezed in my direction. What should be my response to your inexplicable absence of expression? How should I understand it? I crave but a morsel of your affection, Jamz, but if I cannot have it, could you not at least spare me a tiny paring of your scorn?

If you cannot spare a heap of disdain, I would settle for a snack-size portion of pity. I feel certain you would bestow at least that much on me if you could see me now, for I am a miserable sight. The day is cold. The day is wet. A pelting rain has soaked me through. Adequate shelter is plentifully available, but I am in a mood to have my psychic state and my physical being embrace one another on the same low ontological rung. That is why I have exposed myself, like Lear, to the elements and abandoned myself to wholesale drenching. I squat in the shadow—or what would be the shadow, were the daylight sufficient to allow one—of the memorial to Jean Pezon: a striking and imposing monument depicting a brave fellow straddling a fearsome, roaring lion. If it is an eccentric example of funerary portrayal, it is also apt.

Pezon—as you may know, Jamz—was a celebrated lion tamer. The big cat he wrestles, here in the 86th division, was his beloved sidekick, Brutus. What is not evident from their posture of bronzed permanence is that Pezon met his end when the situation was reversed, and the lion happened to be on top: a position, Jamz, with which you are no doubt familiar. No one can say why Brutus did what he did. Perhaps he was having an off day. Perhaps he remembered some niggling grudge: a thorn that stayed too long in his paw, his abduction from the grassy savannah of his childhood. Perhaps, at a critical juncture, instinct simply ran roughshod over affection. Whatever the case, it was clamp of jaw, swipe of paw, and Pezon met the lion's maw. I suppose that, as a cat, I ought to invest a certain pride in the jugular evisceration so nimbly effected by our jungle relation. However, I am bound to say that I feel a greater kinship with the poor sod who lies beneath this sodden sod; for I know what it is to be slain by the Brutus one loves. *Et tu,* Jamz!

Now, as the rain hardens into sleet and the north wind grows rank with the smell of failure, I remember all the enticements I have latterly lobbed in your direction. I have suggested a sunset stroll through the scenic Jewish quarter. I have offered to introduce you to my friends and to make you presentable by grooming you so that you look less like a tomcat ready for a rumble. And I have volunteered my services as a masseur, night or day, any old time you feel like receiving a full-body rubdown. None of these blandishments, seemingly, has meshed with your needs.

I ought, I suppose, to abandon hope, but I still have sufficient optimism to dangle one more carrot before you. I wonder, Jamz, if a night at the theatre might strike your fancy? I have, with some difficulty, secured two excellent seats for the Renaissance Revue, and if you would care to be my escort, I should be very pleased to have your company. I think we would cut quite a swath, Jamz, and I daresay you would benefit from the absorption of a bit of culture. As well, there are sure to be cats in attendance with whom you are familiar, or have been familiar. With some, I gather, you have been very familiar indeed. In fact, I do believe our seats are located directly to the front and to the right of Colette, with whom I believe you are fleetingly acquainted. She will be very pleased to see you, I know. Very. Do say you'll come, Jamz. Do. Awaiting whatever word you care to send, I am your ever faithful, ever hopeful,

O.W.

❧

ALICE B. COOKS:

THE DOVE THAT DARES NOT SPEAK ITS NAME

Now and then one meets those for whom compromise is, they say, anathema. Such steadfast souls wear their self-proclaimed rigidity as a badge of honour. Their refusal to compromise, they say, has nothing to do with a vaunted sense of self-worth or a perverse fondness for being just plain difficult. Rather, it is meant to signal a disinclination to settle for the ersatz or to put up with second best. As for me, I have never been averse to adjusting my standards to accommodate the reality of the moment. Such flexibility, I find, greatly reduces the rolling of eyes and the gnashing of teeth, both of which are deleterious in the long term. It is a very good thing that I have developed so laissez-faire a posture. Consider the following, just in from Sarah Bernhardt:

Dear Miss Toklas:
The Renaissance Revue planning committee has reached a compromise solution that we hope will satisfy both of the firms shortlisted for the catering contract. While we have engaged the other agency to provide the comestibles for the after-show buffet, we would be very pleased if you would agree to furnish an assort-ment of tasty snacks for the intermission. I do hope you'll see your way to clear to accepting this assignment and not take it in any way amiss.
Yours very truly, etc. etc.,
S.B.

And so Héloïse begins her triumphal march, with the devoted Abélard as her little drummer tom. She must be ever so pleased. I cannot say that I wish her all the best, for she, above all other cats in Père-Lachaise, makes me want to check the spelling of "conniving." Nor, however, am I unduly upset. I think the theatre adage that there are no small parts, only small players, is equally applicable to the catering business. In any case, I have plenty to occupy me just now, what with my charitable work and those private clients who still come calling.

"I was hoping, Miss Toklas," said Oscar, "that you might prepare a picnic supper, a light repast that I could serve to a friend before the revue."

"Any special requests?"

"I'll leave it to your discretion. The one thing I would say is that my guest tends towards the taciturn, and if you could devise something that might prime the conversational pump, I'd be grateful. Something to set the talk flowing, perhaps to enliven the synapses which, in this case, seem to have atrophied from lack of use. In other words, Miss Toklas, the gustatorial equivalent of a bolt of lightning."

"Leave it with me, Oscar. I know just the thing."

And I do. And here it is:

Take a dozen doves. Remove their tongues, reserving the rest of the birds for other uses. (The breasts are tasty when grilled, the feet can be made into cocktail picks, or the whole creature can be very attractively dressed by a competent milliner.)

Poach the tongues lightly in a shallow bath of dry vermouth and a squirt of lemon. Cool. sprinkle with bacon bits and a very generous dash of hashish. Serve on a bed of mustard greens.

LA FONTAINE'S VERSIFIED WALKING TOUR: ROSSINI

To ageing well, there is an art,
The art of letting go.
Of freeing from their gilded cage,
The things we'd rather stow.
Of knowing when the songs we've loved
Are better left unsung,
Judiciously abandoning
Such crooning to the young.

For there is nothing quite so sad
As singers past their prime,
Who trespass in some upper range
Forbidden them by Time.

It's true, as well, that getting old
Ought not necessitate
A wholesale turning of the back
Or cutting of the bait.
One need not think the simple fact
Of sagging jowls and tush
Exacts the abnegation
Of the joys of being louche.

For there is nothing quite so bleak
As old folks making nice,
Believing they should not indulge
In geriatric vice.

Rossini is an ancient cat,
Antique, grown full of days.
A checklist of his symptoms shows
He's deaf, he's stooped, he's grey.
His eyes are dim with cataracts,
He suffers with catarrh,
His time upon the catafalque
Cannot be very far.

But he's not catatonic yet,
No catacomb's his cage.
He's finishing his catalogue,
The sins of his old age.

✤

LETTER: ROSSINI TO MARIA CALLAS

December 11

My dear Miss Callas:
I see that I am meant to write to you. It says so on my to-do list: "letter—Miss Callas." That is what I have written, directly beneath the words "to do." Forgive me for asking, Miss Callas, but why exactly am I meant to write to you? Have you any idea? I feel sure I once knew, but now it is gone. I have become a little that way, you know. A little absent of mind.

Who are you, Miss Callas? Your name is very familiar. Are you the one who sends the little blind tom over with such nice grub? If so, then I can only think I must have intended to speak to you about your use of chili sauce. Could you, Miss Callas? Use chili sauce, I mean. I note that right now you don't, at least not in a quantity that it is discernible. I'm sure this oversight is born of kindness, perhaps out of deference to the delicate constitution that is so often the lot of cats who are on in years. Rest assured, however, that I have the stomach of a tom half my age.

How old am I, by the way? I have quite forgotten. But I remember that they called my father "old iron guts" and I have inherited his gift for easy digestion. I may well have passed that boon on to someone, I suppose. You are not my daughter, are you? Perhaps you are! If so, it is certain that you will have a taste for chili, and you should feel free to sprinkle it as liberally on my dinner as you would on your own. I find it warming, you see. I am so often cold.

Or are you the gossipy groaning one who comes to launder my sheets? That may very well be so. I have been meaning to have a word with you for some time now about your use of bleach. I think perhaps you have been rather stinting in recent months, and I would like to see that corrected. I like my sheets to be the colour of blamelessness, and now they are rather more spotted than I think is necessary. I am old, after all, and there are bound to be spots. I cannot help it if I drool at night. Nor is my bladder as retentive as once it was. And the hairballs are something awful this season. So more bleach, please. Pour it on, Miss Callas. Pour it on.

But then again, might you be the pretty little cat who sometimes does her ribbon dance on moonlit nights? If so, I cannot think of a single reason that I would want to write to you, unless it might be to say that I look forward, very much, to the next night when the moon shines full, for it is always a pleasure to see you perform. Sometimes, when I watch you spin and turn, I feel a current in my loins that rarely visits me now. It does me good to know I have not been entirely unplugged.

Or might you be the drama queen with three legs? I half recall that there was a queen with three legs whose company I enjoyed for a season or two. She was very much younger than I, but I remember that we each found the other to be wonderfully willing. If that is who you are, I must have put you on my to-do list because I was invaded by a deep nostalgia for a time when I was full of a hunger you were uniquely qualified to fulfil, and I wanted to write to tell you so. Which now I have done. For all the good that does, Miss Callas. For all the good it does either me or you.

Miss Callas, Miss Callas. Who are you, Miss Callas? Are you the pinch-faced little thing who delivers the mail? Because if you are, I'm in luck. Just now I have looked up to see you coming down the road, hauling your bag behind you. Hurrah! That means I can hand this over to you, *tout de suite,* and you can deliver it to yourself at your leisure. Good! That solves that! What a relief to have come to the end of it! I may be old, but I remain rigorous about taking care of business.

And now that I have satisfied my one obligation for this day, I can do as I please. I can make tracks before that dreadful harridan comes hammering again on my door, screeching about the song she says I promised to write for her. "I have to sing it in two weeks, damn you. Where is it?"

Tell me, Miss Callas, who the devil is that woman? She is demented, poor thing. Who does she imagine me to be? Me? Write songs? For as everyone knows, Miss Callas, I am now, as I have always been, a simple soldier, a humble conscript, with no needs other than a cosy trench to curl up in and no ambition other than to hear the comforting boom of the cannons once again. *Boom! Boom! Boomity-boom!* That's the only song I care to hear. Blood and carnage and derring-do: it's all just merriment to me, Miss Callas. All just merriment to me.

And now I really must be on my way. Somewhere, there are battles to fight, campaigns to wage, and heaven knows I'll never find them by dallying here. So, good day to you, Miss Callas. I am happy to have written. No response is necessary, for who knows when it might reach me? I have no forwarding address to leave behind, there are no *poste restante* possibilities, and who knows where I'll be or how long I'll be gone? Who knows? God is the answer, Miss Callas. God only knows. Now, all that remains for me to do is to check you off my list. There! See? I have done it. Now, it is over. Now, at last, I am free to go.

I remain, if only in memory,
Private Antonio Croce-Spinelli,
Infantryman, 71st Division

P.S. I see that there are a few pages of music which have been left on my table by someone called Rossini, whoever he might be. I have used some to wrap up my sandwiches. If the mad diva wants the others, she is welcome to them.

ALICE B.

Rossini is dead. Oscar found him. He was far from home—
Rossini, I mean—recumbent at the base of the statue of the

Good Shepherd, curled trustingly in a posture of easy repose, nose to tail. Oscar reported that, viewed from above, he looked like something that had been too long overlooked in a confectioner's window: a sugar cookie, say, or a meringue.

Poor Rossini. He must have been wandering. Wandering, whether in body or mind, was his chief occupation in recent years. It was very usual to see him out and about, rambling here, rambling there, with neither agenda nor destination in mind, simply wandering and singing the songs he loved to sing, the old songs, many of them the songs he wrote, once upon a long time ago. He would sing them in his pleasing, gravelly voice, sing the melodies, at least. The words were long forgotten. *"Bum-dum-diddle-um-dum,"* he crooned. *"Bum-dum-diddle-um-dum."*

There was no hint of anything sinister in his leave-taking. It was a passing past due; a gentle death, or so we hope. It appears that, mid-wander, while resting in the shadow of the statue of the Good Shepherd, he was touched by the Muse of napping, whose visits he has latterly been accustomed to receive. He lay down at the feet of Jesus for a little catnap and closed his one eye on the world. We like to suppose that he never so much as stirred, never felt the slightest shift when dreaming relinquished him to death. There he lay, and there Oscar found him. Rossini at rest. White as a lamb. Stiff as a board.

I will miss him, the hoary old warrior, the sweet-tempered Cyclops. I will miss his tuneful syllabifications, miss the jaunty way he would hold his twin hearing trumpets to his ears, swinging his head back and forth in elephantine arcs from one interlocutor to another, scooping up as much of the chat as he was able, which was never sufficient for him to sustain the thread. I will miss the cubist nature of his conversation and his easy way with non sequiturs. "It all comes down to noodles," he might say, when the talk was about weather or rheumatism.

I will miss the casual way he would extract his false eye and polish it by rolling it around in his mouth before carefully reinserting it, often with the painted iris staring into the cavern of his skull. I will miss the way he would laugh at a joke to which he alone was privy, miss how he would then wink complicity, forget that he was winking and panic momentarily when he believed he had gone blind.

I will miss his polite inquiries after the state of my bowels, and the long, detailed descriptions of his own copious and fragrant movements. I will miss the way he would show up in unexpected ways and places, fully convinced that he was where he was meant to be but always cheerful when informed otherwise, always willing to be redirected or escorted home, where he would not remain for long. Most often, when he appeared, he was simply folded into whatever activity happened to be underway.

"I only hope," I recall Oscar saying, not many weeks ago, "that I will be able to avail myself of the afflictions of age as well and as selectively as Rossini." And it was true that Rossini often turned his dementia to his advantage. It was astonishing how often his seemingly random arrivals at my own door, for instance, coincided with mealtimes.

"Not again!" Tristesse would sigh, whenever Rossini's signature William Tell knock would punctuate the air just as we were sitting down to eat:

Whack-a-whack
Whack-a-whack
Whack-a-whack-whack-whack!

"Don't answer!" she would plead, for she found his visits deeply unsettling. His unstinting ways when it came to second and third helpings, his habit of talking volubly while he ate, and the masticatory spray that blew from his lips during his windy expositions, always put her off her feed.

"Ladies," he would inevitably ask, slicing the nose off the brie and pressing it into the heel of a baguette, "have I ever told you how I lost my eye?"

"Often!" Tristesse would answer, with a desperate look in my direction. I could only smile and shrug, for Rossini was not for turning.

"Ah! I can see you are surprised. Many people find this news incredible but, yes, yes, it is perfectly true. I have but one eye. Look. I will prove it!"

"Please don't," begged Tristesse, for she knew what was coming next.

"Voilà!" And out he would pop the prosthetic orb from its socket and set it on the table between the cheese and the fruit, where it looked calmly into space, an all-seeing grape.

"It's a beauty, is it not? The great Géricault himself painted it for me. He did a bang-up job, I'm obliged to say. A bang-up job. I know people who say they would give an eye for a Géricault, but I'm the only one ever to have done exactly that! Ha! That was rich, if I do say so. Have I ever told you how I lost my eye?"

"No! Please, no!" Tristesse would beg, but Rossini would not be deterred. It makes me sadder than I can say that we will never again be his captive audience. Now, for the record, I shall set down the preamble to his tale, which was his predictable party piece. He told it so often, and the rhythm and cadence were so much a part of his being, so integrated into his circuitry, that it was exempt from the otherwise wholesale erosion of his memory.

"What do you see when you look at me, my kits, my cats, my dearest dears? A vessel full of days. The house where stiffness lives. The nest where feathered memories come and go, come and go, singing their tuneful, empty songs. Look at me and what you see is Rossini, the happy sinner, hauling the yoke of all his wrongdoings behind him, but never complaining, merrily wearing the heavy mantle of all his grievous misdeeds. You see Rossini, grown old and cold but glad he was bad. Bad, bad, bad. Yes. Very bad.

"The pious among us take great umbrage at such a wanton admission. They shake their heads and say, 'Rossini, you are old. You are on the wane. It will not be long before you meet your maker. Would you not like to wipe clean the slate?' Wipe it clean? When what is written there is so titillating? To do so would be a crime against history! Against literature, even.

"Wipe clean the slate! What a notion! I, Rossini, am ashamed of nothing. What have I done that imperils my soul? To the accusation of randiness, I plead no contest. I have been lusty all my life. What of it? Were it not for the wide-open spaces of my heart and the steamy overflow of my loins, many of those who now see fit to upbraid me would not be walking on four legs through the world. And though some of those same scolds would call me 'glutton' before they would call me 'father,' I prefer to think of myself as one whose mission has been to play host to every possible hunger.

"I have explained all this to the adherents of the straight and narrow, but they will not abandon their windy insistence that first one must disown the past, and then one must atone for it. Nothing short of an eye for an eye and a tooth for a tooth will do, as far as they are concerned. In fact, I have sacrificed more than one fang on the black altar of so-called gluttony. And as for an eye—well, have I ever told you how I lost my eye? No? Have I not? Well, then, I shall."

It was at this point that consistency met its end, and the story veered off into any number of variations on any number of themes. Duels, games of chance, the spiked heels of careless chorines, pirates on the Barbary coast: all could easily figure in his gory accounts, and the whole while he talked, Tristesse would squirm, the eye itself staring into the void from its place on the table, an unblinking centrepiece.

"Where is my eye?" he would say, when he had finally told all there was to tell. "You have it there? Thank you. See? See how easily it fits back in? You'd never know it for a fake. Is there dessert? And coffee would be lovely, thank you. Brandy? Yes, surely. Then perhaps I can tell you the story of how I lost my eye."

Dear Rossini! How I wish you might have hung on another

month or two. I should have liked you to meet Gertrude, for I know that you would have loved one another. But now you are gone, gone for good, leaving us with memories and sadness and, as it turns out, a small mystery, too.

"I suppose you heard about Rossini's eye?" Piaf asked today, when she made her usual Wednesday washerwoman stop. It was the question of one who derives great satisfaction from being the first on the scene with an especially moist morsel of gossip.

"No. What about it?"

"You ain't heard?" she replied, thrilled at my ignorance. "Jesus, girl! Where've you been?"

"What?"

"It's gone. His glass eye, I mean. Plucked right out of his dead old head. Vanished. Bonne Maman is beside herself. She's ranting all up and down the boulevard about how she's sure that the same son-of-a-whore who stole her book is behind the theft of Bernhardt's leg and the disappearance of Rossini's eye."

"Why would she think so?"

"Says that they're all needed for some love spell. Says that whoever's on the make is wasting his time, because he'll never get his paws on the power source. Says she has it under lock and key."

"Power source?"

"Beats me, Miss Toklas. I didn't ask any questions. Now what the hell kind of stain is this, then? Raspberry? Where the hell do you get raspberries this time of year?"

Dear Rossini. Gone, but not soon to be forgotten. Gone, but possibly not for long. Whatever legs and eyes go missing, whatever spells are cast and miscast, still the cosmos keeps on spinning around and spitting out the numbers for the reentry lottery. I wish you a safe and eventful journey. I wish you an easy and speedy return.

❖

CHOPIN: NOCTURNE FOR THE FEAST DAY OF ST. LUCY
(INVOKED AGAINST EYE DISEASE)

Who has stolen Rossini's eye?

That was the only inscription on the unsigned card I delivered up to Proust, yesterday afternoon. Yes, yes, I read his mail, and yes, I am embarrassed to admit it, though of course I intend no intrusion. I am, as Postmaster, scrupulous about safeguarding the privacy of the mail. But the carelessly cobbled collage of words caught my attention, and before I could avert my glance, I had taken them in, my brain had apprehended their sense, and I had, against my will, breached my pledge of confidentiality:

Who has stolen Rossini's eye?

"Ho, Proust!" I called and rapped firmly on the iron portal of his mausoleum. Hammering hard is necessary, for he is notoriously difficult to arouse, especially when he is lost in his meditations, his special brand of hindquarters speleology.

"Ho, Proust! Open up! Post for you!"

He must have been very enmeshed indeed, for I heard a

sound of slow suctioning, as of a cork being pulled with painstaking care from a bottle, then a long sigh, and then his sluggish shuffle as he moved to the door, which—after unfastening its many latches—he opened a crack.

"It's you, Chopin."

"It is. And it's you too, Proust."

"That is so. I am very much myself. More so than ever, in fact. To what do I owe the pleasure?"

I passed him the card through the narrow crack.

"Surely you're not delivering the mail yourself these days, Chopin. Where's the girl?"

"Tristesse? Who can say? Her work habits have become somewhat erratic of late. She's taking part in a play, you know, and I rather think it's all gone to her head.

"The Renaissance Revue?"

"The very one. It's an annoyance, but it'll be over soon, and then she'll either revert to her dependable ways or she won't. If the latter, I shall be looking for a new letter carrier."

"Ah," said Proust, reading the message on his card. "Perhaps I should apply."

"What? Is the P.I. life too wearing?"

"You smile, Chopin, but I am having an exceptionally busy season. Strangeness walks among us. You have heard, I'm sure, of the recent rash of thefts."

"I've been aware of some talk, yes."

"And now this: *Who has stolen Rossini's eye?*' "

"It is very curious."

"It is very maddening. If this keeps up, I shall have to install one of those waiting-room machines that dispenses numbers just to keep track of my petitioners. Goodbye, Chopin," he said, as he closed the door, "and thanks for your good work."

That was yesterday. Perhaps tomorrow I shall route myself by Proust's place again and pass on to him the details of my last night's dreaming, which may have some bearing on his most recent case. I dreamed I was walking through Père-Lachaise. It was nighttime. The dark was deep and still.

I was quite alone. Even so, I knew I was observed. I looked left, looked right, looked all around. No one. No rustle of leaf, no sound of footfall. No telltale whiff of musk or perfume. And yet, incontestably, I felt between my dreamtime shoulders the disembodied weight of another's steady regard. Finally, I looked skyward. Then I saw it, Rossini's eye, suspended up above, pinned to the overarching blackness, caught like an inflated blowfish in the spiky net of stars. Rossini's eye, occupying the very place the moon ought properly to have hung. Rossini's eye, wide and unblinking, round and floating, drinking it all in. Every coming and going. Every nook and cranny. Every secret of every heart.

I saw the eye. The eye saw me. I was certain, with that strange surety that belongs only to dreaming, that if I could just stare back at it long enough, if I could only best it in a contest of unblinking persistence, that its painted pupil would open, and everything it contained, every image and story, would pour from it, like honey from a comb, would coat me, would enter me, would fill my vacant spaces.

I snapped awake from my dream before any such spillage could take place. I rose from my cot and went out into the night, St. Lucy's night. Dark and deep and still, it was exactly as I had dreamed it. Déjà vu! I tilted my head, slowly, and noted—half with relief, half with disappointment—that no eye was in view and that the moon was exactly as it ought to be: full and white, pocked and waxy, its chill luminescence uncompromised by anything other than some wispy emblems of transient clouds and the nervous silhouettes of the now-and-again bats.

It is a pity that the night guards are the only upright walkers to see Père-Lachaise by moonlight, for there can be few places on earth where the vistas are so enhanced by lunar illumination. A towering marble angel; a spooky mausoleum or mossy stele; the verdigris-streaked bust of some bearded and forgotten worthy balanced atop a granite plinth: nothing is quite so delightfully garish, so perfectly clichéd, as funerary monuments viewed in the mysterious half-light cast by an obliging moon.

Mind, even on nights when the moon has withered to a jaundiced sliver, or on nights when the sky is so thickly overcast that not a single star is in evidence; even then, we cats can see as readily as when the sun is shining. The nocturnal world loses none of its diurnal clarity if you have protean eyes that shift to accommodate any available light. Were I to compile a catalogue of the ways I have been compensated for the loss of music, night vision would lead the list. True, it is a gift that is universally held among cats and is in no way particular to me; but like every other commonly bestowed boon, it has been doled out in greater and lesser degrees; and, as always, there are those who find ways to turn it to their advantage.

At night, as my eyes penetrate the dark, I sometimes feel as though I am creating a unity between two worlds, between the tangible and the imagined. At night, it can happen that my fancy will engage with the dark in such a way that I am able to look within and without at exactly the same moment and to erase the border between those two principalities. It is at moments like this, when what lies within and what lies without are projected simultaneously onto the same screen, that revelation, however minor, is at hand.

Last night, as I looked into the dark and sifted through the remnants of my Rossini dream, I was visited by a low-wattage glimmer. Whether we prance through life on four legs or plod along on two, the situation is exactly the same. The pair of eyes is fixed in place. They look out. They look around. But never, ever, do they look back on the house in which they live. We are never able to see ourselves as others see us. Only when we die and the flesh relinquishes the soul can we finally look down upon the clay that contained us and appreciate the full effect of our physical presence. By then, typically, we are not looking our best. The open mouth. The lolling tongue. The stiffening limbs. The eyes that register alarm. Nothing about it suggests peace or redemption, only horror and intense discomfort. It

is exactly the same look that seizes the countenance of someone who is slipping on a banana peel or who has just taken
delivery of a large dropping from a passing fowl. Really,
laughter is the only appropriate response.

There I sat, under a sky with no eye, musing on how the
complexion of our beloved Père-Lachaise might be different
if the two-legged living understood the intrinsically farcical
nature of the post-mortem experience. Would these gorgeous
acres have been consecrated to such lovely, overwrought
expressions of longing and loss, of sadness and sentiment?
Would there be so many monuments to dynastic aspiration: all
these lavish family mausoleums, all these miniature palaces,
and no one to dance in them but skeletons? Would there be so
many graven representations of weeping and mourning? I
suspect if the newly bereaved knew that Papa would eventually
reappear—but with four legs and a tail, velvet triangles for ears
and sporting a calico waistcoat—that funereal architecture and
decor would be a good deal less, well, funereal.

All the sculptures of tearful babes, of sombre angels and of
grim-faced spirits struggling to extricate themselves from the
chill embrace of marble would be supplanted by memorials
that were gayer, more whimsical, more practical, even. Yes! It
would be the perfect opportunity to blend the useful and the
amusing. Why not commemorate one's sister or cousin or aunt
with something that might provoke a smile and at the same time
have some earthly utility, such as a scale that gives both accurate
weight and a printed horoscope? Or why not a tanning bed, a
drinking fountain, a bubble gum—dispensing machine?

"What's so funny, Chopin?"

It was Isadora, out at all hours—as always—who invaded my
meditations.

"Funny?"

"You're giggling, my darling," she said, laughing herself as
she pirouetted past, on her way back from Lord knows what and
en route to heaven knows where. "Sitting alone in the dark and
giggling. You want to be careful, or you'll get a reputation."

"I already have a reputation," I answered, but she was gone, claimed by the night. That is her way, just as it is the way of every waking dream and every living eye. Just as it is the way of every single puzzle you ever think you've almost solved.

LETTER: ISADORA DUNCAN TO MODIGLIANI

December 17

Dearest Modi:
All I can goddamn well say is, if the way you keep your goddamn appointments is anything like the goddamn way you'll be as a goddamn daddy, then it's a goddamn good thing I'm not counting on your goddamn support when these goddamn kittens get born and give me back my goddamn body. Which can't happen goddamn soon enough, by the goddamn way.

Goddamn! I'm ticked off, Modi. Where the hell were you today? Didn't I see you just last night? And didn't I say, "See you tomorrow, okay"? And didn't you say, "Yeah, sure"? And didn't I say, "Miss Toklas is expecting us at three, right"? And didn't you say, "Uh-huh"? You said it like you meant it, Modi. So what gives?

Me, I got there right on time. Miss Toklas was fussing around in her kitchen, like always. The portrait was up on the easel. Of course I wanted to take a peek, but it was covered up with a sheet.

"How's it look?" I asked.

I felt shy about asking, though I couldn't tell you why. Right away I felt bad that I'd even brought it up, as if I'd burped when I should have swallowed. But hell, don't I have the right? It's me who has to sit for hours on end while you eat piece after piece of her fudge. I don't know how you can handle that stuff, I only ever tried it once, and for days afterwards the world looked to me like a half-finished jig-saw. It's my face you're messing with while you're downing that stuff. It's my face you're making long or short or purple or green or whatever the hell you're doing. A hundred years from now, when this thing is hanging in some goddamn gallery somewhere, it won't be you they'll be looking at, but the me you see. So why should I pretend that I'm not interested? But Miss Toklas wasn't for it.

"Better you should wait, Miss Duncan. Wait until he's done. There's an energy at work. It would interrupt the flow if you were to look into your own eyes. It's bad luck for a subject to see a portrait in progress. But please, accept my reassurances that your friend is doing a beautiful job."

Why would I doubt it, Modi? Everyone knows you're good. What I want to know is, why are you so damn unreliable? You put me in an awkward spot by not showing up. You know how much I hate small talk.

Finally, the door opened, and, of course, I thought it was you. But no, it was just her halfwit sister dragging her mailbag behind her.

"Miss Duncan, you remember Tristesse, don't you?"

"Oh," the sister said and took a step back. She had this look on her face I couldn't quite read, half surprise, half anger. The dazed look of a sleepwalker who's just been woken and still has a foot in the country of dreaming.

"Sorry, Mademoiselle Alice," she said. "I didn't realize you had company. I thought you'd be out." She began to back out the door.

"You know I'm never out on Tuesday afternoons, Tristesse."

"Tuesday?"

"I believe it's Tuesday today. Miss Duncan, is it Tuesday?"

I nodded. I might not be the world's brightest light, but at least I know what day it is. Unlike some, Modi.

"Tristesse, what on earth is in that bag?"

"Parcels."

"Parcels?"

"Lots of parcels. Big day for parcels."

"I'll have a word with Chopin. It's not reasonable to expect you to haul around such a load."

"No! I mean—don't tell—it's just that—I mean—please."

"Tristesse, whatever is wrong? Perhaps you should have a little lie-down."

"No! I can't. Parcels. Mail. My lines—I have to practise my lines."

"That's absurd, Tristesse, you don't have any lines. Miss Duncan, did you know that Tristesse has been give a role in the revue? It's non-speaking, of course, but pivotal all the same."

"I really have to go now. Really. Goodbye, Miss Duncan."

And off she went, with her bag thudding behind her.

"My apologies. Tristesse is a nice girl, but she's never fully recovered from her birth."

Who has, Modi? Who has? I wonder if these goddamn kittens will ever get over theirs, please let it come soon.

"Miss Duncan, you are looking rather thin, especially given your circumstances. Won't you stay for dinner? I'd wager you could use a good meal."

Jesus, Modi! I swear that old queen lives to make us fat! It's eat this and eat that and eat the other thing. It's nibble, nibble. Every time I leave her place I have to make myself puke. I'm a dancer, Modi, and I'm not going to let myself get all plumped up, goddamn kittens or no goddamn kittens.

"Thanks, Miss Toklas. I'd better just get out of your hair."

"Will you come for another session tomorrow, then, Miss Duncan?"

"Yeah. Sure. I'll tell Modi."

And so now I am. I'm telling you. Tomorrow, Modi, okay? Wednesday. Three o'clock. Miss Toklas's place. I want to see you. I want to see me, too. The me you're painting. The me in your eyes.

Yours,
Isadora

ALICE B.

Sometimes—perhaps at four in the morning, perhaps at eleven at night—I enter the nebulous no man's land that lies between waking and sleeping. Then, as the receptive mind shuffles from vibrant to dormant, I am visited by the grainy recollections of another inanimate interlude, a longer and subtler season of suspension. In such tabula rasa moments, I might remember a time which is no time at all, a placeless place free of every temporal and spatial vicissitude. Which is the place where she is now, my love, my puss, my Gertrude. Which is the Waiting Room where one lingers after one's two legs have given out and before one's four legs are assigned. All memories of that transitional place should be purged at the moment of translation. Even so, I recollect the lowery, sulphurous light and a dense, leaden silence, broken now and again by a voice, clarion yet calm, matching names with places, such as one might hear in a busy train station: *Miss Toklas, Miss Toklas, leaving now for Père-Lachaise.*

And then here I was, and now here I am, no longer in the Waiting Room but still waiting, as it turns out. I am waiting still.

Gertrude Stein, Gertrude Stein, I'll keep waiting till you're mine, waiting till you come to me, waiting, waiting patiently. What can I say to urge you back, what reassurances can I offer? I can tell you that life on four legs affords many pleasures; that a cemetery—contrary to what one might believe—is full of event. Here one rediscovers, slightly reconfigured but nevertheless in spades, the same pleasures that animated our two-legged lives on the rue de Fleurus, on the rue Christine. There are friends and there is Art. There is gossip and there is food. And, praise be, there is smoking.

"Fetch me some tobacco, will you, Tristesse?" I asked my sister when she left the house this morning. "I'm nearly out."

"You shouldn't—" she began, but I silenced her with a dismissive wave.

"We've been there before, my dear. No need to visit again."

"It's not good—"

"I know very well what's good for me, Tristesse. I know what's good for you, too, so please uncurl your lip. It's most unattractive."

Tristesse's Calvinistic petulance is one of her least appealing qualities. Whenever I light up, she makes an elaborate show of flapping her apron to shoo the aromatic phantoms from the room. Or she'll unleash a volley of wheezing sighs that always puts me in mind of the bagpiper who once made an appearance here, kilted and sporraned and otherwise equipped with the monstrous appurtenances of his trade. A man with a filial mission, he stood before the tomb of an ancestor who had come to grief on French soil and proceeded to rend the air with pibroch after mournful pibroch. It went on for hours. *Très, très désagréable.*

"Tobacco, then," Tristesse answered coldly, reaching for her mailbag. "Anything else?"

"Chestnuts. And please stop by the drugstore to see if there's any hashish available. I'd like to make some fudge."

"N-n-n-no, Mademoiselle Alice!" she stammered, letting fall her sack before collapsing to the floor in a melodramatic exhibition of prostrate horror. Our life together has always been enlivened by such displays, but never more so than in these last few weeks, when the theatre has been much on her mind. Tristesse, to her own astonishment, and certainly very much to mine, has been chosen to take part in our upcoming pageant, the Renaissance Revue. Indeed, she will be playing no less pivotal a role than that of the bumbling junior acolyte in "The Sorcerer's Apprentice," a *tableau vivant* that has long been a staple of those proceedings.

My sister owes her impending debut—and a more unlikely occurrence you could hardly imagine—to the political manoeuvring of a faction within the planning committee that oversees the revue. After considerable internal wrangling, the committee decided to make a concerted effort to involve the untranslated in their annual production. The official line for such a shift, which has been highly controversial, is that "We must broaden our audience base and strive for greater inclusivity." My own guess is that it has more to do with drumming up interest in a tired tradition than it does with a democratic exercise; but perhaps this is just an ember of cynicism glowing at the heart of my being.

And how did Tristesse became a pawn in the game? Certainly not by putting herself forward for consideration. Rather, in the show-business way of things, she happened to be in the right place at the right time. She turned up at the door of the Palazzo Phèdre with a routine delivery, and Sarah Bernhardt, seized by who knows what inspiration, pegged her for the part. Tristesse is so compliant that it would never have occurred to her to say no. She saves all her adamant refusals for me, her sister.

"Get up, Tristesse, and don't make a spectacle of yourself. I need you to stop by the drugstore. It will only take a moment."

"I can't! You know I can't!"

I have no need to inquire after the reason for her reluctance; for while tobacco is easy to come by here at Père-Lachaise—this is France, after all, and there are stray cigarettes everywhere—the one reliable outlet for hashish, the place I fondly call the drugstore, is an address Tristesse cannot abide: the final resting place of James Douglas Morrison.

"Final resting place." The halting vocabulary of the mortuary is full of such pale palliatives: toothless nostrums patented by the living to mitigate the prospect of oblivion. One is not long sundered from the flesh before one learns that there is nothing final about dying and not much that's restful, either. Morrison's grave, a case in point, is about as peaceable as a Sunday afternoon at the Louvre. Day after day, hundreds of his disciples flock to render homage to their avatar-gone-to-dust, proffering the usual tributes: flowers, guitar picks, candles, photographs, uniformly bad poetry and, with delightful regularity, a thoughtful assortment of mild hallucinogens. Oscar and I, when we are in the mood for bread and circuses, will sometimes sit at a discreet remove and watch the milling masses. Oscar unfailingly offers a breathless commentary on the teeming pilgrims, particularly on how they are costumed and coiffed.

"*Regardez*, Miss Toklas. Here comes a parade you don't want to miss, a glorious gaggle of grotesques, and all with matching thatching. I've rarely seen so much hair with so much heft. What kind of fixative would be required to achieve that topiary effect? If only I knew, I might be able to do something about your bangs, Miss Toklas. Have I spoken to you about your bangs?"

"Often, Oscar."

"Oh my goodness! Speaking of hair, here comes a bird with some dazzling plumage. A veritable rainbow, Miss Toklas. I haven't seen such a collation of colour since I fell face forward into a pastry trolley at Blackpool. And what a display of hardware! Ring upon ring. You could tie a thousand ships to the left ear alone."

"Do you suppose it hurts?"

"But surely that is the point, Miss Toklas. Why do it otherwise, other than to give the wind a place to pass through? Shhhhh! What's this now, clanking along? So many chains, like Marley's ghost, only more comely. And now he is turning around, so that we can consider him from every angle. Oh, Miss Toklas, shield your maiden eyes."

But it was too late. I looked. I saw the gaping holes in the seat of his trousers.

"He'll catch his death of cold, Oscar. Should we organize a charity drive to buy him some drawers?"

"Perish the thought, Miss Toklas. Perhaps I'll just rub up against him. That would be warming."

Sophomoric, to be sure. However, a distraction is a distraction, and I welcome any anodyne that eases the pain of the waiting game. That Tristesse is unable to wring anything like delight from this daily carnival is, I suppose, my fault, and my fault alone. She has no independent memory of the cannibalistic melee that blighted her first day on earth, but I

have so often told her the story of that primal bloodbath—
graphically emphasizing the Lizard King's savagery and my
own heroic intervention—that she has incorporated it into
her personal mythology and cannot so much as hear
Morrison's name without her heart lurching and sputtering
to a near stop. Trips to the drugstore, therefore, are always
fraught with imagined peril.

"No, Mademoiselle Alice," she said again. "Not there. Not
him. Don't make me."

"Snap out of it, Tristesse. I've told you time and again that
you've nothing to fear from Morrison, not as long as I'm in
the picture. He's no more liable to hurt you than a hawk is
likely to swoop down from on high and carry you off."

I said this by way of emphasizing the absurdity of her fears,
but I could tell from the way her eyes bulged that I had only
succeeded in sowing the seed of yet another worry.

"Send Buttons!" she pleaded.

Which I suppose I could easily have done, but I was in a
mood to let it be known that I was still the boss.

"Buttons is busy. In any case," I said, handing her the
mailbag, "you have a delivery that will take you there."

At this she gaped anew.

"What do you mean?"

"There's a letter for Morrison."

"How would you know?" she asked, her voice crimped with
suspicion.

"I happened to see it last night, after you'd gone to bed."

"You were snooping through the mail again?"

"Tut-tut. I meant no harm. I was hunting down the salt
and I'd looked everywhere else."

Tristesse is the living embodiment of gullibility, but even
she, under normal circumstances, would have scoffed at so
flimsy a comeback. In the moment, however, the unsettling
news of the missive for Morrison had loosened her hinges,
which are never too securely riveted.

"Who's it from?"

"Who do you think?"

"No!"

"I'm afraid so."

She grabbed up the bag and rooted inside.

"Oh," she said, as she took in the name of the sender and the return address. "Oh," she said, and her poor little face took on such a look of dejection that I was almost moved to embrace her.

"Dear Tristesse. I have so often told you that Oscar is not an appropriate target for your affections. You must understand this by now."

She nodded, mutely, and returned the letter to her bag.

"It's just that—"

"No, Tristesse. For any reason you would care to name, it would never, ever, work out. Now, tell me again what you're to bring home."

"Tobacco," she answered, affecting a posture of crestfallen resignation. "And chestnuts."

"And?"

She sighed the sigh of the deeply defeated and mouthed the third of her commissions.

"*À bientôt*, Tristesse."

Alone at last. I sat. I listened. Rain on the roof. The braying of a magpie. In some distant quarter, the whack of mallet on chisel and chisel on stone as the name of a new tenant was added to some familial roster. Otherwise, nothing. All quiet. I emptied the last of the tobacco from the humidor and tamped it into my favourite pipe, longing for the day—oh, let it come soon—when Gertrude would be here to lean over and light me up, first in one way, then in another. In her absence, I went to the window where burns the perpetual flame, the symbol of my certainty. I leaned into the candle, engaged the fire, drew in the sweet residue of burning leaf. Then, as if there weren't already a surplus in the neighbourhood, I filled our house with ghosts, and then with ghosts again, and then again with still more ghosts.

❖

La Fontaine's Versified Walking Tour: Ondine

Oh, kittens! What miraculous embodiments of joy!
They're chubby, cheeky cherubs: cheerful, comely, cute and coy.
Their mothers, while astonished that such beauty here
 abounds,
Admit that kits are pains right where the gluteus is found.
Their appetites are fathomless, one cannot plumb their guts:
When suckle turns to fecal, there's the licking clean of butts,
Which isn't appetizing, but ensures that they will thrive
To live to play another day when mother's sleep deprived.

Although they view their progeny with wonder, love and pride,
All mothers whisper once, at least, the word "infanticide."
At least once in her lifetime, I'd bet every mother here
Has voted for Medea as the "Woman of the Year."
The pressure! It's imperative to garner some release,
To find a way to colonize a tiny patch of peace.
Some subterfuge is *de rigueur*, and every mom subscribes
To certain clever stratagems, inducements, threats and bribes.

Practitioners of parenting, whatever else they preach,
Know "treat" is simply "threat" without the benefit of "h."
Treats and threats can both end spats and bring on spates of
 calm:
If proffered bonbons fail, there's always smacking with the
 palm.
Whatever works, I always say, and what works hereabout—
When kittens get all querulous and spit and fret and pout—
Is whispering, "Ondine, Ondine," oh nemesis most foul:
Ondine, Ondine, she's mean and lean and out and on the
 prowl.

"Now hush," the worn-out mothers say, "and neither squeal
 nor cry—
Ondine is in the neighbourhood, she hunts for us nearby.

She's eager, but she's patient, lurking still as any stone,
Her sacks are poised and empty and she won't go home alone!
So quiet, now. Be quiet, now." And all the turmoil ends:
As muted kittens drift to sleep, a welcome calm descends.
Both benison and bogey, that's Ondine's twin purpose here.
The mother of tranquillity. The fodder of our fears.

LETTER: OSCAR WILDE TO JIM MORRISON

December 19

Dear Heart:
That is what I call you, Jamz, but I have begun to wonder
whether you have a heart at all. I see no evidence of it.
Indeed, I have begun to wonder whether I might have fallen
victim to my brain's inconvenient penchant for unpremedi-
tated anagrammery. Is it possible, Jamz, that you are not
"Dear Heart" at all but, rather, "Rare Death"? I have come at
last to think so. I have died a thousand deaths, Jamz, each one
rarer than the last, with your every snub. But now it is over.
Done. Finished. Listen. Do you hear that rustling? It is the
sound of a veil being drawn.
    I have not managed to make myself even an inconvenience
to you, so I think you will find no relief in learning that this
is my last letter. You will not hear from me again. There still
lives in me, buried deep beneath my shredded hopes, a small
remnant of self-respect. Before it is snuffed out altogether, I
will call a halt. You must know how I feel, Jamz. How could
you not? And yet, your carapace is so granite clad and your
brain so evidently lizard like that perhaps I have been too
subtle in my barrage. Perhaps I have erred in not saying out-
right that I love you. So now I say it, baldly and clearly: I love
you. I do. But to what end? Unless love finds a welcoming

heart, it is no more electric than an uncompleted circuit, no more effective than a poltergeist without a dusty attic where it can make its noisy presence known. So, I give up.

My one last gift to you is a warning, my dear heart, my Jamz, my own rare death. Beware of Ondine. You must surely have noticed that she is here every day now. Indeed, she is here into the night, skulking in dank mausoleums, concealing herself when the guards make their rounds. She is the incarnation of dark purpose, snatching whomever she can, and you know whom she most longs to nab. I hear her as she snakes among the headstones, muttering her "Come to Mama, come to Mama, do" exhortations.

"Viens, viens, viens à Maman, viens mon beau, mon mec à trois boules."

So watch your back. Do not underestimate her. She took Modigliani only yesterday, and someone as cagey as he could not have been easy to catch. Nonetheless, he is gone.

His abduction was the cause of some considerable social unease just a few hours ago, at the home of Miss Toklas. I had gone there for a card party, a small *fête* in honour of Chopin, who, after years of patient gathering at the grave of Mademoiselle Lenormand, has finally managed to amass a full deck. It was he who answered the door when I rang, and I have never seen the melancholy Pole cat quite so happy, quite so kittenish, even. He swept me up in a little waltz and sang a silly ditty of his own composition:

A tom of many parts
Requires a suit of hearts.
And, good friend, by your leave,
I'll wear mine on my sleeve.
No need for waxing glum,
My queen has finally come.
Three cheers! Hip, hip hurray!
And a rum-bum-diddle-aye-day!

Isadora was also in the room, which surprised me. Miss

Toklas hadn't mentioned she would be part of the company.

"Why, Miss Duncan. So nice to see you. Are you joining us for cards?"

"No," she said, rising up from her chair with a flutter of ribbons, "no, I was just on my way out."

"Oh, do stay, Miss Duncan," said Miss Toklas. "We could use a fourth, I'm sure. Chopin, what's the inaugural game to be? Whist? Bridge?"

"Hearts, I think. Miss Duncan, do you play hearts?"

She smiled a slow and foxy smile that made her look more shark than cat and betrayed that she was as adept at gambling as at gambolling.

"Hearts? Why, my dear Chopin, I would rather shoot the moon than yowl at it."

"Ha!" he cried and began to shuffle. "I do believe the gauntlet has been thrown!"

Dear heart, rare death, in my more lunatic moments, when I let my fantasies get the better of me, I imagined the day when you would be my companion for such jolly outings. Now I see that this will never happen, and perhaps that is just as well; for truly, Jamz, what good would you be at a game where the object to give away the heart? What would you know about such a thing? Unlike Chopin, whose heart was dispatched to Warsaw. Unlike Miss Toklas, whose heart is on long-term consignment. Unlike me, whose case you know. And unlike Miss Duncan, whose heart is also spoken for. If only I had known about Miss Duncan and the owner of her heart, I would have been more temperate in my revelations.

"Tell me, Miss Toklas, what's that?" I asked, as she busied herself setting out snacks.

"What's what?"

"There, in the corner. Covered by that sheet."

It was Isadora who answered.

"That," she said, "is a sore spot."

Then she went on to tell of how Miss Toklas had commissioned Modi to paint her portrait and that they had waited for him all afternoon and that he had not appeared.

"It's the second time he's missed an appointment," said Miss Duncan, who was considerably riled, "and I'll have a thing or two to say to the bastard the next time I see him, you can count on it."

"You mean you haven't heard the news about Modi?" I asked.

"What news?" asked Isadora, and I should have guessed by her tone of voice that he was something more to her than a hired portraitist.

"But I thought everyone knew! Everyone's talking about it."

"Knew what? What's happened?"

And I blurted it out. When I finished my story, the name Ondine hung in the air, floating in the charged silence. *Ondine, Ondine, Ondine.*

At the very moment that Miss Duncan rose from her chair and opened her mouth and shrieked out her horror at what I had so blithely imparted, the door of Miss Toklas's house was flung open with a force that fairly tore it from its hinges and tossed it into the room, followed by—all spit and hiss and irrational carrying-on—a tumbled and tousled amalgam of fur and fury.

"Where the hell is it?"

Bonne Maman!

"Where? Where? Where?"

Her yellow eyes were rolling back in her head and her fur was sticking out at every angle.

"Which one of you *putains* has it?" Her voice was hoarse with rage. "Out with it! Which one?"

Miss Toklas stood up. "Madame, I wonder if you might perhaps—"

"Get stuffed!"

"—have made an error—"

"I said get stuffed! You know what I'm after, and if you don't have it, one of your friends does. You!" she bellowed, pointing directly at me. "You took it, didn't you! You always wanted it back, you nutless coward, and now you've taken it. You can't have it, it's mine now! Mine! Give it to me!"

She grabbed hold of the table and upended it as easily as if it were a stale rusk. Cards flew everywhere—a scatter of bad fortune—and Miss Duncan, dazed by the news I had just imparted and caught unaware by the force of the witch's projectile, was knocked to the floor. The table crashed down upon her.

"No!" cried Miss Toklas, then "No!" again as Bonne Maman laid hold of the sheet that covered the portrait and pulled it free.

"Where!" shrieked Bonne Maman. "Where, where, where!" And she flew from the room as gracelessly as she had entered, trailing the sheet behind her, a very unsettling ghost.

Watch your back, Jamz. Watch your back. These nights are full of intrigue. Watch your back, dear heart, for whatever sneaks up on you next will not be me. Not me, rare death. Never again will it be me.

O.W.

Letter: Colette to Jim Morrison

December 19

Sir:

In another life, in another time, in the disappeared days of that upright long ago, before I understood, proprioceptively, what it would mean to own whisker, claw and tail, I would often practise exercises of deep empathy—for empathy is the midwife to all literature—and imagine how life would be if one lived it as a cat. Indeed, I recall that I tossed off a novella called *Le Chat*, a slender, charming study of lust, jealousy, possessiveness and murderous intent. Always write about what you know, and in those days I surely did know what it was to be a slave to those emotional masters. Evidently, I know so still.

Morrison, Morrison, why have you forsaken me? How can you pretend that I am nothing to you? I know you were not unmoved by what passed between us. I heard your moans, saw the rolling of your eyes, felt the clench of your teeth, the throbbing of your loins. One look at me is all it would take to prove that your intentions were, in the moment, serious.

I am grown huge, Morrison. Huge! I look like an outlandish deity, a minor fertility goddess whose adherents offer only the gift of refusal. You, sir, are not the only one to be so withholding. Just this morning, my yoga students staged a Gandhian show of civil disobedience and refused point blank to assume a very gentle, pelvis-expanding position.

"Forget it," said Callas, speaking the mind of the group.

"It will do you good," I said, but my pleadings were for nought. None of them so much as stirred. They simply remained on their backs, lowing gently, their limbs and tails arrayed in various postures of abiding discomfort.

I could tell that no amount of cajoling would change their minds, and so I did a shameful thing. I gave in and joined them in their gravid lassitude, and slipped almost immediately into a strange and satisfying trance. In my altered state, I entered my own body, as if it were a country separate from myself. I went walking through its luscious landscapes, a happy wanderer singing "val-de-ree, val-de-ra." I came to a sun-dappled glade—a dreadful cliché, but there you have it, that is exactly what it was—and who should be sporting there, playing at hoops and quoits and horseshoes and hide-and-seek, but six pretty kittens! And I knew, even though we had never been introduced, that they were the kittens I carry. The kittens you made, sir. In case you had forgotten.

"Darlings!" I called, but they seemed not to hear me. On and on they played, oblivious to my presence, caring only for their games.

"But are you not going to come and kiss your very own mother?"

And it was at this point that reality intruded on my charming fantasy, reality in the guise of Bernhardt's foot, or perhaps all three of her feet, nudging me repeatedly in the ribs while she hissed, "For God's sake, Colette. Get up! Get up!"

Cold consciousness splashed me from my trance, as subtle as any icy spray, and then came those words again. But it was not my lips that shaped them. It was not my voice that spoke.

"But are you not going to come and kiss your very own mother?"

"Christ, no!" I shrieked, involuntarily, then tried to suck back the words, as if they were errant noodles spilling from my lips. I hauled myself into a sitting position, rising up with all the certainty of a novice chef's soufflé. I blinked hard, three times. I looked into my own mother's icy blue eyes.

"*Chérie!*" she trilled, and in a trice she was all over me.

"*Maman!*"

"I've come, *chérie*, just as I promised I would. What mother would not move heaven and earth to be with her daughter in her hour of deepest need? To say nothing of agony. I remember when you were born. Terrible! You were breech, you know. Searing, ripping, rendering! Don't believe for a second the nonsense they spout about how you forget the pain. I'll remember it till the day I die. Not that I would have had it any other way, of course. I must say you're looking rather huge, *chérie*. It was different for me. I ate and ate and hardly put on an ounce. You have a different metabolism, obviously. It was very sensible of you to simply give in and pack on the pounds. You'll have a job to lose all that fat after the babies arrive, but why worry about that now? Just relax and let Maman tend to your needs."

Had she, before I was born, studied her own mother and considered her ways? Had she given herself a stern talking to and said, "I will never be as she is?" What instinct takes over and obliterates every mediating influence of tact and discretion?

"*Chérie*, you know that I've never been given to interfering. You know that I've always been supportive of your choices, however *outré* they have been. But now I feel I have a responsi-

bility to speak my mind, frankly and with all candour. Do you
really think that this place—which is not without its charm, I
hasten to add—is an appropriate environment for the raising
of my grandkittens? Come home with me, Colette. Back to
the rue Benjamin Franklin, where you belong. You are, after
all, a Persian. There are standards to which you must adhere.
And really, *chérie,* while I think of it, why on earth have you
allowed your fur to become so matted?"

So it went, and so it will go. Now, mercifully, she is asleep.
I had forgotten how loudly she snores. She will awake refresh-
ed and eager to begin in earnest the battle of my repatriation.
This is one skirmish, I can promise you, that she will not win.
Return to the 16th? I wouldn't last a day. I need my inde-
pendence, and, what's more, I need the possibility of
romance. I had hoped, sir, that you would be its glad
provider. Now I know this cannot and will not be. There is
nothing left to say but fare thee well. It won't be long, I daresay, before some more willing and accommodating tom
comes along to darken my door.

That's the world for you. It is full of shadows. Some we
welcome, and some we fear. Some we endure and some we
simply choose to forget. Which brings me to my final word,
Morrison. It is goodbye. You will not hear from me again.

C.

LETTER: ISADORA DUNCAN TO MODIGLIANI

December 20

Dearest Modi:
I looked. It wasn't my fault, you know? I didn't mean to, but
still I looked. So much was happening, so much goddamn
noise and commotion, what with Bonne Maman shrieking

and Wilde whimpering and the table falling on me and then this burning in my groin.

In the middle of everything, I looked up, and there was the sheet that had covered the painting—it was floating away, but in slow motion, like a goddamn ghost in no hurry to get anywhere, and I should have remembered what Miss Toklas told me, about not looking at it, about bad luck and all. I should have thought, but I didn't, and I looked, Modi. I looked. I looked right into my own eyes. My gaze met my gaze. I saw me the way you see me. I saw that you think I am beautiful.

"No, Miss Duncan!" Miss Toklas cried as I dragged myself across the floor.

Five, Modi. That's how many I carried.

"You must stay quiet."

Five, and I didn't want to spill them there. I needed to get home.

"You must rest. You must—"

But there was no "must" for me except the must of my own body, and my body had taken over by then and knew that what it had to do was dance. That is a dance I hope never to dance again, that dance of seizing and crawling; for a dance should be about reaching up, about reaching out, and this had nothing to do with up or out. And instead of reaching, there was retching, only retching.

Five, Modi. That's all I can tell you, other than that they were tiny. Other than that they were dead. And Jesus, but it hurt. Jesus.

I guess you know a thing or two about hurting, too, don't you, my Modi, sweet Modi, poor Modi. What's the lesson of all of this, then? Is there a lesson? No, unless maybe it's that nothing will ever be the same again. And what kind of a lesson is that? No lesson at all, really, since that's the one thing we can be goddamn sure of, isn't it? Nothing will ever be the same again. What does it all mean, Modi? My best guess would be not so very much at all.

Did Ondine give you a return ticket? I sure as hell hope so.

Come to me when you can. You know where to find me. You know that in the end, whatever happens, it all comes down to two things. Number one: the show must go on. Number two: I love you.

Isadora

✤

CHOPIN: NOCTURNE FOR THE LONGEST NIGHT

It happens every year, just around now, that the sun grows tired of being taken for granted and decides to take his golden ball and go home, flouncing off into the west by 4 o'clock. Luckily, these fits of pique are short lived. By dawn tomorrow, if the familiar pattern holds, he will already be casting furtive glances back in our direction. We will offer a few conciliatory words, and it won't be long before we have, once more, his undivided attention:

> *Shine, friend sun,*
> *Shine blood red.*
> *Shine on the living,*
> *Shine on the dead.*
> *Shine on two legs,*
> *Shine on four.*
> *Shine till night comes,*
> *Shine once more.*

Typically, the music that comes to me during this season of deepening dark is cast in a minor mode. Sad. Reflective. Suffused with the certainty of ending. The melodies are marked with sluggishly cautionary indications: *largo, andante, grave*. This year's musical offerings, however, have been uncommonly uptempo—indeed, some verge on *allegro*—and more than a few have been in the optimistic major keys of C,

Modi's portrait of Isadora

G and even E flat. I welcome such goads to briskness, for
there has been no slowing of the midnight mail, and a march
or mazurka helps me maintain the pace. There will soon be a
plenitude of birth announcements to sort and deliver, and,
of course, there has been the usual seasonal onslaught of
cards and packages. As well, we have had the additional
encumbrance of an unexpected mass mailing. The culprit is
the following chain letter:

Dear Friend:

*This comes to you with love and the sincere wish that it will bring you very good
fortune. In order for luck to come your way, the letter must not stay in your pos-
session for longer than forty-eight hours.*

*Georges Bizet took this seriously, and, within days of fulfilling his obligations
to the chain, a whole flock of starlings fell from the sky and plummeted down his
chimney, straight into his empty cooking pot.*

*Less than a week after scoffing aloud at these requirements, Georges Seurat
was seized by a peregrine falcon and dropped to the pavement from a great
height, a tumble worthy of Icarus that reduced him to a series of teeny tiny dots.*

*This letter has now circulated thirteen times around Père-Lachaise. It orig-
inated with the celebrated gastronome Brillat-Savarin, who distributed the first
copies at an elaborate dinner party, intending it as a diversion to occupy his
guests between the twelve courses of their meal. Do not be deceived. The letter
may have begun as an amusement, but its efficacy as an engine of fate, good or
ill, has been amply demonstrated over the years.*

*Loie Fuller complied with the requirements and had a litter of five spry kit-
tens, three of whom were translations: Guillaume Apollinaire, Yves Montand
and Isadora Duncan.*

Send a copy of this letter, unsigned, to ten friends or acquaintances.

ANONYMITY IS PARAMOUNT!

Sarah Bernhardt ignored this clause. Within a week, she had lost her leg.

*In order for luck to come to you, you must embrace your task with love and
goodwill.*

*Abélard grumbled the whole time he made his copies. Within a week, he had
fallen into the hands of Ondine, and duplication of any description was, for
him, no longer a possibility.*

Simone Signoret, conversely, was full of excitement and charitable purpose while she made her transcriptions. Very shortly thereafter, she was awarded a leading role in the Renaissance Revue.

Coincidence? You decide.

Happiness, success and fertility can easily be yours! Disaster, misery and dismemberment can just as readily come your way! It's up to you.

Good luck, friend.

You now have forty-eight hours to keep the chain unbroken. The clock is ticking. The future is coming fast.

It's an annoyance, this letter, but not unexpected. Cats are, by nature, a superstitious bunch, and our occult tendencies become all the more pronounced during flood tides of fecundity. One does what one can, in such circumstances, to roll out the red carpet for good fortune. Exactly what constitutes good fortune, when it comes to birthing a litter, is an interesting study. No expectant queen will come right out and say that she is hoping there will be a translation or two among her brood. To do so would be unseemly and would also jinx the possibility. Nonetheless, it is exactly what they do wish, some of them quite fervently.

Piaf, who has her ways of ferreting out such information, passed some on to me the other day when she came by to launder my smocks. Maria Callas, she says, aspires to Bellini or Charpentier. Sarah Bernhardt is hoping for a Rothschild. And it was revealed to Colette, in a dream, that she is growing heavy with Beaumarchais.

"As for Miss Toklas, who's not even knocked up and never going to get that way, she's got her hopes up that her Miss Stein will come sliding down any old chute at all. She doesn't care! Christ, I sure do hope she gets here this time around. I don't think I can stand another season of moping."

I note, with interest, that no one aspires to be the mother of Victor Noir. Indeed, as near as I know, he has never once been translated, which seems a pity. He would surely have a lot to say for himself. He certainly did during his brief years of walking upright, which ended in 1870. He was a crusading journalist and just into his twenties when he was shot dead by Pierre Bonaparte, who had taken umbrage with some acerbic aspect of Noir's editorial stance.

Death has a way of conferring on certain people gifts and responsibilities that they never hoped to own in their lifetimes. For instance, it was never my ambition to become a cat, nor did I ever aspire to become Postmaster General. Nevertheless, *me voilà*. Likewise, there was nothing about the life of Victor Noir—nothing that was ever reported, in any case—that presaged his candidacy for the role he now plays, which is that of fertility fetish. It is Victor, or rather his bronze effigy, that makes the 92nd division one of our necropolis's most visited tourist destinations. There he rests: young, handsome, dead and in considerable disarray. Dalou, who was commissioned to craft the monument, shows us Victor in the immediate aftermath of the shooting. His shirt has been unbuttoned, presumably by his friends, in order that he breathe the easier. His trousers are likewise unfastened. His top hat lies at his feet.

This all makes sense. Less discernible is why Dalou chose to endow young Victor with a vigorous and visible member. You needn't look twice to see it, for he is spectacularly tumescent. One wonders why the Parisians of the day—who only a few years later were shocked by Oscar's petsie, which was made of stone but was nonetheless flaccid—would allow such an indecorous swelling to pass scrutiny. Scrutinized it was, and it did not take long for word of its swollen prominence to spread near and far, and for a ritual to develop.

For generations now, women have journeyed to Père-Lachaise to caress the sculpted bulge and to ask the passive but priapic scribe's intercession as they begin the pilgrimage towards motherhood. Victor has been rubbed so often and so fervently that his trousers have acquired a lustrous sheen. On sunny days, the glare is quite blinding. And even on cold days, the constant friction keeps the bronze warm. There are times—I have seen it more than once—when the faithful bestow on him more than a casual pat. I have watched women straddle him as they might, say, a hobby horse, and rub themselves lasciviously against him; a manoeuvre presumably favoured by those who are in excellent shape or who are desirous of multiple births.

What was Dalou's purpose in casting so cheeky a detail? Perhaps he meant to underscore the link between death and eroticism. That connection has often been noted, theoretically, but no one could live in Père-Lachaise for long without acquiring a practical understanding of how it is so. The gravid state of many of my cohabitants should be proof enough, and many two-legs have discovered that a cemetery such as ours is the ideal setting for the mating of sex and mortality, the regenerative and the degenerative. Père-Lachaise, to speak frankly, sees a tremendous amount of upright action. I daresay that the city of Paris is fairly crawling with citizens who were spawned behind these walls: who were seeded in quiet corners or in the sheltering shade of a chestnut or in a disused mausoleum, as loins pressed to loins against a cool sarcophagus, with no one but a stained-glass saint looking on.

What will he be like, Victor Noir, should he be among the cookies in the many batches now baking? Will he live up to the promise of his bronzed manhood? If so, he might well give Morrison a run for his money. I, too, might find myself in competition with him, for Victor has links to the post. Visitors are forever leaving prayers and billets-doux in his top hat. Perhaps if Victor arrives, trailing behind him those strands of awareness, he will choose to devote himself, as the quintessential male, to the disbursing of the mail. I wouldn't try to intervene. In fact, I would welcome the chance to step back from my quotidian labours. "It's up to you now, young cat," I would say, and then retire altogether. I could relax. Sleep in. Travel. Perhaps I could go to Warsaw to visit my heart.

Oh! No sooner do I speak those words than I feel an unsettling lurch in my left chest, as if my here and now heart had stumbled at the prospect of such a reunion. Heart, heart, jealous heart! Settle yourself. You know that the better part of me is talk, only talk. Be calm, old heart, and save your strength for what's to come. Somewhere overhead, well out of sight and floating above us with consummate ease, good fortune and ill luck look down on all of us, and laugh as they study their cards.

✤

ALICE B.

It won't be long now, Gertrude, my love, my puss. Any day now, we shall see. Any day now, if all goes as I pray it will, when the pageant has ended and the due date has come, and the heaving and shoving are over and done, then I shall go out to find you. I will know you when I see you, when I look into your eyes and that small bell rings within when one translation meets and knows another. Eye will meet eye and the bell will chime, and lo, it will be you, and I will know and you will know, and the future will begin.

Appearances count for nothing, but of course I am curious to find out how you will be wrapped. Will you be stout? It will be of no consequence whether you are or whether you are not, but I confess that it will make me very pleased if stout is how you turn out to be. In that other time and that other place, when we walked upright in our other bodies, then you were my fine stout husband and I was your loving wifey, and your stoutness was part of what I loved and will love again if stout is how you are. No matter, though. I will love you stout and I will love you thin. I will love you round or narrow, squat or lean, bent or straight, or white or black or tan or grey or any combination and permutation pertaining thereto. I will love you then as I have loved you always, which is exactly how I love you now.

However you are packaged, I will adore and admire you. You craved admiration, always, and you will be pleased to learn that in this place, for our kind, it is not in short supply. You will quickly learn that Père-Lachaise is full of upright walkers who chirp, purr, mew, smooch and otherwise beckon us.

"Oh, look," I heard one suddenly sentimental fellow say to his friend not so very long ago, as I was passing by at a distance, skirting one perimeter or another. "Look over there. Doesn't she look like our Babe? Doesn't she look like Babette? Kitty! Kitty! Here, kitty-kitty-kitty!

I have grown accustomed to such mawkish manipulations and never resonate to them, but in this case I did at least stop and give him a long and considered regard. Babette! It gave me a frisson, I can tell you, for that, of course, is what that B is for; the B in Alice B. Toklas. I have been Miss Toklas for so long now that I had quite put it from my mind. I had quite forgotten the B. Forgotten that B is for Babette.

B is for Babette, and that's not all. B is for Beloved, and B is for Betrothed, and to me you are both. B is for that, too. B is for Both.

B is for Birth, and B is for Born, and when you have had your Birth, my Betrothed, my Beloved, we will be Both be together in this beautiful world.

And B is for Buttons, whom you will meet, and who came hurrying to find me yesterday, not long after he had set off with his meal delivery for Proust. I was in the thick of helping Tristesse with some last-minute adjustments to her revue costume: a cape all appliquéd with stars and moons and planets, very wizard-like. It was clear that Buttons was agitated, and he made it known through a series of signals that I was to follow him.

"Not now, Buttons," I said, articulating as carefully as I could, for my mouth was full of pins, "I'm very busy."

This was not the first time that he has made such a request and presented it with the same dancing urgency. But whenever I have trailed along after him, the revealed root of his concern never has never measured up to his air of fevered necessity. Indeed, the last time, he wanted only to share his high hilarity at the sound of a cellular telephone chirping in the marble confines of a sarcophagus in a family mausoleum. Evidently, someone had recently been interred in a suit with a pocketful of portable; or else his family had left it with him in the event of a sudden revivification, so that he might summon help. And while I smiled in the moment—imagining the would-be interlocutor, waiting and waiting to hear a voice forever stilled—I was not, just then, while fussing with Tristesse, in the mood for such diverting hijinks.

"No, Buttons!" I said again, but he was not to be deterred. Finally, I gave in and followed him down his secret staircase into the catacombs. This airless anteroom to Hades would never be my first choice of destination for a pleasant promenade, but it was a relief to secure, even in this way, a break from the black cloud that is my sister. Tristesse has always been prone to sulkiness and petulance, heaven knows, but in these last weeks she has become even more sullen and somewhat secretive. I attribute this to anxiety over her impending stage debut and look forward to the day—soon, now, very soon—when the revue is over and she can return to being conventionally unpleasant.

We hurried along for some minutes, skirting sticky pools of specious goo and dodging all manner of ossified oddments, tailings that a keen anatomist would love to name. I had no idea where we were going, nor did I know at first where we were, when we surfaced into a sarcophagus and stepped into a dark and silent room.

My cat eyes quickly adapted to the absence of light. I saw a table, piled with paper. A few dishes, carefully stacked. A narrow cot, neatly made. And tossed upon on the floor, incongruous in its careless casting, was what I took to be a funeral wreath: one of those garish ceramic rounds that have become so much in vogue in recent years, exempted as they are from the inconvenient business of wilting. It was to the wreath that Buttons drew my attention, circling it by way of a nimble step dance, like a maiden prancing around a maypole. I looked closer.

"No!"

Buttons nodded.

"It can't be!"

He nodded more vigorously still.

"Proust?"

Buttons nodded confirmation and signed to me the story of his discovery. He had knocked at the door, received no answer, grown concerned, then utilized his underground entrance—and discovered the private investigator arranged in the posture in which we saw him now: that is, a joined circle, his head completely absorbed by his posterior crevice.

"How on earth—"

Buttons motioned to the table. Next to some piled papers, a card:

Who has stolen Oscar's Petsie?

I took the top leaf from the pile of paper. I sat on Proust's cot. I read:

And now the time has come, as that time always must, when all the parts of the equation have been revealed and all that remains is to undertake their tabulation. How best to add, subtract and divide

> *—a book of spells*
> *—Bernhardt's leg*
> *—Rossini's eye*
> *—and now, a limestone petsie?*

"Something big is going to happen, I tell you. Something big!" was what the witch Bonne Maman hissed at me when she hammered on my stolid door, pounding it with the crackling violence of a lightning storm.

"If some amateur tries to power up that petsie, Proust, there's no telling

FRANCE 3₅₀F

what might happen. All that's certain is it won't be good. So you'd better track it down, Mr. Smartass Detective Cat, because we'll all be lost if you don't."

Eventually, she left, and the silence she had displaced returned, but her desperate need was still palpable in the air, and I knew that she was in earnest and that I must act, and act quickly; and I knew that it was in the heart that I would find the answer, for there is nothing the heart doesn't know. So I lay down upon this floor, my ear pressed to the marble, and I listened, as though through the humming lines of a switchboard, for the sound of every beating heart, for the two-syllable truths they contain and will always tell. I heard "Come soon, come soon" and knew that it belonged to Miss Toklas. I heard "I want, I want," and recognized the wail of Wilde. I heard the tuneful "Fa Sol, Fa Sol" and understood that I had connected to Chopin. I listened harder still, listened for each voice in the chorus:

Me too, me too.
Be strong, be strong.
Screw you, screw you.
I long, I long.
I'm here, I'm here.
In flood, in flood.
Be near, be near.
Ker-thud, ker-thud.

One by one, I heard each heart, heard its deepest, simplest songs, and knew to whom each belonged; knew them all save one, one heart only eluded me, swam under my net, one heart held in a cage so tight and with a purpose so masked that I could not, no matter how hard I listened, match it with a face, a name.

Be mine.

That is the song that that heart sings.

Be mine.
  Be mine.
    Be mine.

So, that is who we seek and that is who we must find. The thief who has stolen the leg and the eye, the book and the petsie, is she or he of the secret heart, the heart that beats "Be mine."

And from my own left chest comes that low, familiar bidding: "Go deep, go deep, go deep." And I understand its message. The solution will never be found in this world. It lives only in the heart. How deep am I willing to go to find the truth? How deep am I willing to go to find where every answer lives? Now, I shall find out. Now, I am going. Going now. Going. Going deep. Deep. Deep. Deeee—

I knelt beside Proust. I listened to his heart. I heard it: slow, faint, but steady. It seemed to me to say, "Got you. Got you. Got you."

I don't know what to make of it all. Whether Proust will ever find the answer, whether he will ever emerge, is one more thing only Time can reveal. Poor old Time! So much is riding on him. He has so much to show. His yoke is anything but easy.

B is for Burden and B is for Being. Be here soon, Gertrude, my love, my puss. Till then, I am only waiting.

❧

Presenting

THE 99TH ANNUAL RENAISSANCE REVUE

Columbarium Theatre

December 24

PART ONE

1. Overture, by Georges Bizet

2. Hommage à Rossini

Miss Callas sings a selection of his songs and arias, including the famous
"Cat Duet." (Miss Callas will perform both parts simultaneously,
a daring feat never before essayed.)

3. Kittens on the Quay

Miss Duncan performs an Interpretive Ribbon Dance set to sea shanties.

4. This Fecund Season

Scenario by Colette, starring Sarah Bernhardt as the Maternal Urge, with
Colette and Maria Callas as Ladies-in-Waiting.

Intermission

(Snacks by Miss Toklas)

5. Didactic Dactyls

La Fontaine presents his comic verse, "Stain is only satin with the a and t
reversed," while Madame Piaf demonstrates effective ways to remove
ink spots from an array of delicate fabrics.

6. Hey Diddle Diddle!

Celebrated Père-Lachaise fiddlers Ginette Neveu and Stéphane Grappelli
mix it up with a variety of tunes and styles.

7. The Sorcerer's Apprentice

Scenario and music by Paul Dukas, starring Sarah Bernhardt as
the Sorcerer, with Loie Fuller, Jane Avril and Simone Signoret as Senior
Apprentices, and introducing Tristesse as the Junior Apprentice.

Gala Reception

(Catering by Héloïse)

Programme Correction:
Due to unforeseen circumstances, Miss Duncan will be unable to perform.

CHOPIN: NOCTURNE FOR THE FEAST DAY OF ST. STEPHEN

Dear and blessed St. Stephen, first among martyrs, I thank you for the gift of this cold, long night, this night of many cries. In every division of Père-Lachaise, as if on cue, queen after queen discharges the kindled contents of her womb and lets fly her inarticulate song of agony and exultation, of wonder and disbelief, a dense and riven tone poem.

Dear St. Stephen, you whose holy portfolio includes the guardianship of horses, I remember how, in Poland, on your feast day after Mass, we would shower the priest with oats in tribute to your equine patronage. I remember this and wonder if, in a playful mood, you might have had a word with the keeper of all weather and sent us this heavy snow as a wry reference to that wild scattering. Down it falls, in the still and the dark, with the hushed, dry sound of a filling granary or an emptying urn.

Dear St. Stephen, sentenced by Caiphas to die under a hail of rocks, and whom bricklayers and masons claim as their patron—grudgingly sharing your mercies with stallions and mares—I wonder if you might have room beneath your spreading aegis for critics; critics who, believing themselves without sin, like to cast the first stone. I still remember the names of the vandals who, in the days of my music-making, spat on my work and scandalized my name. Fetis, who found my piano playing too thin for his taste. Rellstab, who wrote that my compositions should be torn into bits. It is the sad lot of those who are brave enough to walk through Art's dark forest that, behind every tree, lurks a marauding brigand. On the other hand, as long as one is not the object of the barrage, there is a certain grim pleasure to be wrung from reading the words of a reviewer who comes to his task with a cross, hammer and nails at the ready.

A critic—and I thank my lucky stars that I don't belong to that cynical fraternity—would certainly have had a field day with this year's Renaissance Revue. He would have begun by remarking on Sarah Bernhardt's bottomless capacity for both involvement and self-involvement ("death-defying megalomania performed without the aid of a net or any restraint"); then gone on to make satiric hay with Bizet's overture ("a tepid casserole of well-masticated tunes"), with the overly strenuous performance of Miss Callas ("what she lacks in musicality and technique she makes up for in vulgarity of tone and expression"), with the bizarre pairing of La Fontaine and Piaf ("the tandem incarnation of an infinite variety of crudity"), and with the misguided collaboration of Neveu and Grappelli ("a combination only slightly less appealing than acid and base"). About the finale, however, "The Sorcerer's Apprentice," he could only have written with reverential awe: "a demonstration of how a much-dusted knick-knack can reveal facets so new and so sparkling that one believes one is seeing the work for the first time. Unforgettable!"

While "unforgettable" is, almost always, a thoughtless hyperbole, it is, in this instance, apt. The bizarre events of that night will endure forever in the minds of those who bore witness and will surely live on in legend. If I close my eyes, I can summon it back, vividly, image after image.

I see the lovely Columbarium Theatre, see the milling audience (the house is sold out) chatting among themselves during the set change that precedes the culminating act of the evening. They're abuzz with anticipation, both because "The Sorcerer's Apprentice" has long been an audience favourite and because, having enjoyed Miss Toklas's entr'acte *amuse-gueules,* they're eager to sup on the sumptuous post-show buffet catered by Héloïse.

I sense the febrile anticipation as the first chords of the Dukas score ring out through the arcade. I see the curtain rise on the clowder of cats in the cast, frozen in tableau. Loie Fuller and Jane Avril and Simone Signoret are the Senior Apprentices to the Sorcerer. With their mortarboards and stark black gowns—which scarcely conceal the melons of their kitten-carrying bellies—they look like new recipients of minor degrees. They glower fiercely as they point accusingly at the Junior Apprentice, Tristesse, who is decked out in a stunning wrap of royal blue, plentifully festooned with moons and planets and stars. Dominating the scene is the ominous figure of the Sorcerer himself: or, rather, herself, the cross-dressing Sarah Bernhardt in one of her most popular and powerful portrayals. The look of wrath on her face as she prepares to mete out punishment! *Magnifique!* The audience erupts into sustained applause, and, after a suitable interval, Bernhardt steps forward to take a bow. She looks pleased and has no inkling that something is about to go badly, badly, wrong.

No matter how often I review what happened next, the scrolling images lose none of their freshness, surprise or horror. Sarah Bernhardt bows, as low as her swollen belly will allow. Then she rises and steps back to acknowledge the rest of the cast. One by one, they come forward. Fuller. Avril. Signoret. Finally, Bernhardt calls on Tristesse, and the clapping crescendos gently, for much has been made of her participation in the revue and her letter-carrying has made her well known throughout Père-Lachaise. What's more, she has, against most expectations, acquitted herself rather well in her stage debut.

Tristesse looks about with the disquieted air of one who is unsure what she should do next. She seems disoriented, wobbly. Bernhardt motions her to step forward. Tristesse steadies herself and walks slowly to the apron of the stage. She pauses, looks out, and the applause swells again. But then, instead of bowing, she flings wide her wizard gown, a grander and more theatrical gesture than seems appropriate for one who is in a supporting role.

A collective gasp gases from the spectators when they get a good gander at what Tristesse has revealed. A pause as pregnant as any of the present queens hangs in the air as the spotlight plays over the black satin lining of the cape, rigged up with an unlikely array of objects.

A sere and severed leg.
A staring prosthetic eye.
A flaccid limestone phallus.

Stunned silence falls over the crowd, and every mind rattles with the sound of mismatched pieces tumbling into place. A chorus of voices, borne skyward on the wings of interrogative disbelief, whispers her name:

Tristesse?
  Tristesse?
    Tristesse?

But Tristesse is oblivious. She starts, slowly, to spin. She begins, lowly, to chant:

Let my hidden love now shine.
Hear my heart. Be mine. Be mine.

At this point, the discrete and individual images leave off and give way to a melee so garish and confused that nothing happens in sequence but all at once, on a continuous plane, as if in a painting by Brueghel or some other such chronicler of hellish happenstance. Every time I study the canvas—and I have been back to it many times—I discern new and gruesome details. I see Bernhardt try to strong-arm Tristesse towards the wings, but the tabby's not for budging. She shakes herself free, she chants, she spins. And with every rotation, the spotlight catches the painted iris of the staring eye, the lurid heft of the petsie, the exclamation point that is the withered leg.

Now Bonne Maman rushes to the stage, a dreadful howl rising from her guts, and that sets the awestruck audience in motion. Panic rules as they scramble for the exits, but their eager search for egress is arrested by an apparition so uncommon and so unholy that they stop cold and watch in a petrifaction of amazement, as Morrison, who has so far been absent from the proceedings, comes flying, quite literally flying, into the theatre, his three balls whirling, holding him aloft, propelling him forward—more or less forward, he is having some difficulty adapting to this new use of his rudder—like something come to life from the drawing board of a whimsical da Vinci

Morrison is a pulsating package of polydactyl perversity, his twenty-four toes wiggling as he paddles the air. His face displays both surprise and determination, the confused and joyful regard of the recent convert who suddenly knows exactly what it is he wants, even though it is something he never once thought of or ever imagined he might need.

Nothing deters him. Not Héloïse, who tries, too late, to divert the inexperienced heli-cat before he crashes into the tables stacked stem to stern with the food she has prepared for the reception, scattering nosh and ice sculptures and dishes and cutlery. Not Oscar, who throws open his arms in an extravagant gesture of welcome. Not Colette, who, in spite of her bulk, leaps into the air with kittenish abandon, mouthing the words, "Down here! Down here!"

Now Morrison has reached the stage, which, it is clear, is his intended destination. All but Tristesse have fled. She is alone, oblivious to this new arrival, as she continues to spin and chant her rhyme, "Be mine, be mine.

No one tries to arrest the airborne tom as he hovers above her, grabs her by the neck and hauls her up. No one intervenes when, in the eerie glow of the half-lit stage, he rends and tears her wizard gown, hurls it to earth and then, without troubling to land, launches into a demonstration of his one, his only, his always reliable, party trick.

"*Enfin!*"

A shrill cry, and every head turns north, the direction of its source.

"*Enfin, mon beau!*"

And a hundred cats scatter as Ondine gallops onto the stage, with a speed and agility that belie her age.

"J'arrive!" she trumpets, aglow with triumph, like a fiancée of many years who has finally reached the altar. Morrison is so intent on his task that he doesn't so much as throw her a backward glance. He is still in mid-air, still bent on servicing his insensible passenger, still howling with pleasure and driving his point home, when Ondine seizes him by the scruff with her scarred left hand; in her right, she wields a pair of sizable shears. And that is where we shall leave them. That is where we fade to black.

Why is it, dear St. Stephen, that we so seldom in this life get what we want and almost never get what we deserve? Consider the plight of Tristesse, a virgin queen, a creature so timid, so disconnected from the universe of her own body, that she has never once obeyed its inborn biological dictates and come into season, never once answered the raunchy imperatives of heat. No one so innocent should have been repaid with such appalling brutality, and the greater pity is that she can't even take comfort in the knowledge that, however much she suffered, her love spell was, at least, effective. For it was not. At least, not on the intended target.

Tristesse of the modest mien. Tristesse of the lowered eyes. Tristesse who is ever so shy. Who would have guessed that she had the wherewithal to successfully plan and execute not one but four cunning thefts? No doubt pressure will be brought to bear on me to fire her, but I shall resist. She has risen considerably in my regard. Indeed, I am coming to see that she is a very estimable young queen. Very estimable indeed.

And now, St. Stephen, *je vous souhaite une bonne nuit.* No need to turn out the stars tonight, as none of them are visible behind the thick curtain of snow. If, however, you are looking for a task, scouting about for some small deed that will make you feel useful, I have a suggestion. Wait till I'm asleep. Reach into my chest. Lift out the beating, softening stone of my heart. Hold it in your saintly hand. Bless it as only you are able. Throw it at whoever needs it most. Throw it where it knows it wants to go.

❧

This is mine forever

La Fontaine's Versified Walking Tour: The Peroration

You read a book. You turn the leaves. They thicken on the left.
The pages on the right grow light, diminishing in heft.
The volume that you're holding now is listing hard to port,
Which means, of course, we're soon to reach the end of our
   report.
The finish line is now in sight: our gothic graveyard tale
Is just about to peter out, the wind forsake its sails.
I'm pleased that I could be your guide throughout this two-
   month trip;
I'll leave to your discretion, friends, the question of the tip.
And if you live just down the block, or if you're travelling far,
Safe journey home. I'm La Fontaine. Goodbye, now. *Au revoir.*

⚜

Alice B.

As if a junior angel had shredded the wrapping on a present
he'd found beneath the tree. As if the revealed box proved to
hold a snow dome. As if the miniature world contained
within its thin glass skin—miniature for an angel, in any
case—the precinct of Père-Lachaise. As if the angel,
delighted, upended the globe, set it upright again and smiled
to see the myriad flakes tumble down in slow cascade. That is
how much our world has been shaken and that is how much it
has snowed. It snowed yesterday, and the day before yesterday, and the day before the day before. It was snowing last
night when I shut my eyes, and this morning there was still
more snow. All day long the snow snowed down, and now, as
the afternoon hardens its heart against the pleadings of the
light, still the snow is snowing, snowing, showing not a sign
of slowing. It is aberrant and beautiful. As if all the world's a
page, bright and new. Crisp parchment. Unsullied foolscap.

Fool's cap. Here there are no hatters, mad or otherwise, but if there were, I would surely have myself measured for one. For a fool's cap, I mean. Nothing else will do for me now. How could I have been so blinkered? How is it possible that I was oblivious to the rotten smell of conspiracy when the source of the stink was in my very own home?

"Just tell me why, Tristesse," I said to my sister, as gently as I could, after I had bathed her and cleaned her wounds and helped her into bed at the end of that night. The night they are all still talking about. The night that no one will ever forget.

"Because I love him," she said, incredulous that I would need to be told. As if I had asked her why she blew the steam from her soup before she put it to her lips.

"Because I love him. Because I wanted him to love me back."

The oldest reason in the world. The only reason in the world.

"But Tristesse, haven't I told you and told you and told you that it's hopeless? Don't you understand—"

"Don't!" she cried, and erupted into sobs.

"Hush," I whispered, dabbing at the hot lava of her tears, "hush, hush. Drink this."

I gave her a double-strength infusion of my very special herbal tea, then sat beside her and stroked her brow until she drifted into dream. I watched the back and forth shuttle of her eyes beneath their shuttered lids and took stock of my own wide-ranging emotions. What an ill-matched march past of feelings! Shock and horror led the parade, as you can well imagine: the shock of my sister's duplicity, the horror of everything I had witnessed. Mayhem. Rape. Dismemberment. And yet, in the midst of all this, and rising above it all, singing like a lark that flies above a battlefield, I also felt an eerie elation, a febrile anticipation.

In spite of everything, I could think of nothing but how the time of my love Gertrude's miraculous advent was drawing near. Two months earlier, I had taken comfort in the mantra "any week now." Then time passed, and "any week" evolved into "any day." "Any day," in its turn, had given way to "any hour," and as I sat by Tristesse and watched her dream, I reflected that "any hour" would soon shed its skin and become "any minute," and that soon thereafter, my waiting would be at an end.

And indeed, it was on that very night, in the wake of all the hysterics, that the kindled queens of Père-Lachaise began to feel the awful pangs that presaged their confinements.

It took two days for every kitten to be born. We have never seen a baby boom like it. Seventy-three kittens pushed their way into our world in those forty-eight hours. Seventy-three! And those mothers-to-be were not the only ones to labour, I can assure you. Imagine how hard I toiled, tending to the needs of my invalid sister—who is a very demanding patient—and then making my way, like a possessed census taker, through the thickening drifts on the avenue des Acacias, the chemin Grammond, the chemin Lesseps and the avenue Morys. Imagine me wading through the accumulating snow, hauling my basket of nourishing treats, going from home to home, bestowing my largesse and congratulations, mewing merry little welcoming songs to all the new arrivals, my heart pounding with pent-up hope as I looked each one in the eyes.

Such lovely kittens they are, too, all seventy-three of them—but there is not a single translation among them. Not a one. It seems impossible, a confounding of every statistical likelihood; but nevertheless, it is so. I have looked. I have seen them all. I know. After all I have done, after all my work, after all my prayers, Gertrude has not seen fit to come.

For two days after the verdict was in, I was as bleak and as low as ever I've been. A paralysis born of exhaustion settled on me. I could do nothing but mourn, quietly, and tend to Tristesse. I saw no one, other than Piaf, who kept her weekly appointment in spite of the snow and stayed too long, complaining loudly about the challenging stains with which she has latterly had to contend. Chopin has also been by, to check on Tristesse and to deliver a letter from Oscar:

My dear Miss Toklas:

How odd to be writing you, rather than speaking face to face as we have so often done before. Of course, I would rather be enjoying your company, but for the nonce I must be a nurse, just as you must be a nurse, as we both devote ourselves, heart and soul, to our respective patient's wants and needs. I hope that your charge is doing well. Mine makes slow but steady progress. He is taxing, that is for certain, and requires constant vigilance. I never sleep, for I feel compelled to stare at him night and day, day and night, alert to his every whimper and moan, to every opportunity to offer him yet another sponge bath.

I have profited from my enforced wakefulness to reason and reflect about everything that has happened. As I'm sure you can imagine, your sister has been much in my meditations. Poor, dear Tristesse! I knew, of course, that she was fond of me. Hadn't you and I often joked, after all, about her "silly schoolgirl crush"? How wrong we were to tease! I had no idea that her feelings were so profound or that she would go to such extraordinary lengths to win my heart. I am shocked, of course, and saddened to be sure, but I am also oddly flattered. After all, who would not feel prideful at having excited in another such deep, if futile, emotions?

Yes, I am flattered, and perhaps I am also ever so slightly embarrassed. Am I the pot who called the kettle black? For all the months of my own romantic hungering, for the whole time I hunted and hounded my beloved, I levelled at him all kinds of accusations of heartlessness. And yet, now I see that I was similarly dismissive of feelings that were, in their way, every bit as desperate as my own.

When all the dust has settled, when Morrison is properly healed, I hope I will have the chance to talk to Tristesse, to say these things to her myself. And while it might be hard for her to hear, I should like to thank her, too; for surely, it was through her sad agency that my own love has been delivered into my keeping, which is where I have every intention of keeping him. You would hardly know him, Miss Toklas. He is so changed, so docile. Why, it wouldn't surprise me if one day he actually speaks.

You, too, are very much on my mind, my dear Miss Toklas. I am sorry to hear that your no news is not good news. Are you quite sure that Miss Stein has not come? Is there really no chance whatsoever? I have rarely known you to be wrong, Miss Toklas, and I am sure you understand that I mean it as no unkindness when I tell you that I wish, from the bottom of my heart, that you are now mistaken.

But soft! He stirs. I must go. I wish you all the best of luck and look forward to seeing you before much more time has passed.

Yours,

O.W.

P.S. This is indelicate, but I can't refrain from asking. As Tristesse is the last repository of my darling patient's seed, I wonder if there are signs that it took root? If it fell in receptive furrows, she would be the last to nurture it. It is a considerable responsibility to the living embodiment of the end of an era.

I managed a rueful smile when I read dear Oscar's news, for who could have imagined so unlikely a beneficiary to all my conniving? I fed his letter to the flame, then curled up beside Tristesse, my head on her belly. This is a position we often assumed as kittens, and now I derive a peculiar comfort from it. I inhaled her scent and thought of Oscar, happy in his newly established harem of eunuchs. And I felt a twinge of something like pity, of remorse, for the newly emasculated Morrison, whose lusty and violent career had come to such a shuddering end.

I turned Oscar's question over in my mind. In truth, it had never occurred to me to wonder if Morrison's last, dramatic act of interference might have lingering consequences. I listened to the beating of Tristesse's heart: *What if? What if?* I listened to the gurgle of her guts. I heard two words.

"I'm here."

Gertrude's voice.

"I'm here."

Again! Oh my love, my puss, my hubby! There was no mistaking it. Again!

"I'm here."

Rich and resonant. Clear as a bell, a deep, brass bell. She said, "I'm here," and the bell within me rang, and I knew, I knew, I knew. Gertrude, my Gertrude! How could I ever have doubted? Can you forgive me? Forgive me my lapses, forgive me my sadness, for you will come, you will come, you will come after all!

That was yesterday. Now, the new countdown has begun. This time, nothing will misfire. In seven weeks, I will meet you face to face.

Between then and now, I shall stand guard over the kettle where you simmer. I shall lavish on Tristesse more love and care than she would have thought possible. I shall make her fat and happy, so that you may be the same. You will be stout, my love. You will be very, very stout!

Today is New Year's Day. Because it seemed propitious and because I was in a mood to make peace wherever peace was in need of making, I whipped up a batch of fudge—stinting nothing—and left Tristesse sleeping while I struggled through the snow to visit Bonne Maman. I found her in a remarkably yeasty mood and not at all inclined to demand the apologies I was prepared to offer.

"Everything happens for a reason, Miss Toklas, I know that better than most. Everything works out as it should. How is Tristesse?"

"Sore and sorry. Mortified, as you might expect."

"She's lucky to be alive. That was powerful magic she was tampering with."

"What went wrong? Morrison was never the intended recipient of that spell."

"I won't trouble you with the technical details, Miss Toklas. What it all comes down to is that delivery is an Art, like anything else. I only hope she's more careful with the mail."

"Were you able to repair the petsie?" I asked, remembering the sound of shattering as it struck the floor of the columbarium: crash of phallus, rattle of eye, thud of flesh.

"Not a chance. Smashed to smithereens in the big dust-up."

"I'm sorry."

"Not to worry on that account. See that?"

The sorceress gestured to a liquid-filled beaker on a crowded shelf, a specimen jar in which floated three marble-like objects, bobbing up and down like happy holiday swimmers.

184

"See those, Miss Toklas? They beat the petsie all to hell, I can tell you. Say, is there anything you'd like to know? Anything about the future, I mean? It's on the house. Compliments of the season and all."

Bonne Maman seemed quite transformed. I'd never known her to be so accommodating. There was only one question I might have cared to pose, but I stifled the impulse to ask it. I am done with occult meddling, and if there's anything in which I have confidence, for the moment at least, it is the future. I contented myself with wishing her all the very best, and then I made my way home. Home is where I am now. Home is where I shall stay.

Tristesse is still asleep. I will shortly wake her, and then I will feed her until she begs for mercy. And when she surrenders again to sleep—it won't take long—I shall lie beside her. Beside her and beside you, my love, my puss. I shall lie with my head on her belly and I shall listen. I shall listen for your voice, listen for the ringing of bells, listen for whatever news you might bring. I shall listen and I shall wait, as I have done for so long

I am waiting for you, Gertrude. I am waiting for your answers. I am waiting for your questions.